Keith McCarthy was born in Croydon, Surrey. Educated at Dulwich College and then at St George's Hospital Medical School, he began practising pathology in 1985 and has done so ever since. Keith is a Consultant Histopathologist in Gloucestershire where he lives with his wife and three daughters.

PRAISE FOR KEITH MCCARTHY:

'Pacey, well-written medical thriller . . . I had to finish it in a sitting' – Andrew Puckett, author of *Sisters of Mercy*

'McCarthy handles his material with real brio' – *Crime Time*

'A gripping plot, startling twists, and a slam-bang ending add up to a fine thriller' – *Booklist*

'McCarthy lays on the grisly detail with a practising doctor's detached eye' – *Publishers Weekly*

A KISS BEFORE KILLING

KEITH McCARTHY

ENDEAVOURINK

AN ENDEAVOUR INK PAPERBACK

This paperback edition published in 2018
by Endeavour Ink

Endeavour Ink is an imprint of Endeavour Press Ltd
Endeavour Press, 85-87 Borough High Street,
London, SE1 1NH

ISBN 978-1-911445-81-4

Typeset in Garamond 11.5/15.5 pt by
Palimpsest Book Production Ltd, Falkirk, Stirlingshire

Printed and bound in Great Britain by
Clays Ltd, St Ives plc

MiX
Paper from
responsible sources
FSC® C018072

www.endeavourpress.com

Contents

Chapter One

No one knows, and no one will ever know, exactly when Edward Marsham's death began, although its end was precisely timed. He was still alive at eleven p.m., according to the uninterested, burly warder who looked in on him at that time. It was only because he began to fit that Marsham did not die in his cell; although he was supposedly on suicide watch, the warder in charge of him had no love for child abusers and wasn't about to waste his time peering in on Marsham every twenty minutes. Marsham's fit took the form of a grand mal seizure so that his head began banging against the door of his cell. This caught the attention of the warder who, somewhat testily ("What the bloody fuck are you playing at, Marsham?"), came back to the cell at nineteen minutes past midnight. When he looked through the spyhole in the door, he expected to see a close up of Marsham's midriff as he banged with something – he hadn't guessed precisely what – on the door, but all he could see was a twitching leg stretching out across the tile floor towards the centre of the cell. The banging continued even as he looked.

"Shit!"

The warder hit the alarm button.

He had a lot of trouble getting into the cell because of the heaviness of the twitching body that sat against the door, but he was soon joined by two others. They shoved the body aside. Marsham had hung himself. He had done so by ripping off the arms of his shirt, then tying them together and then forming a noose. He had anchored it by tying it around the top hinge of the door. Having achieved this, he had just slumped down, lost consciousness and then lost most of his life.

Marsham's transfer to the Emergency Department at the Royal Infirmary was uneventful, and there he was declared brain dead after the appropriate tests were done, first by an ED consultant, Peter Sulston, and then by Claire Woodforde, a consultant in intensive care medicine. He was still fitting, although this had been reduced to a gentle tremor by an injection of intravenous benzodiazepine followed by a supplementary dose in a drip. The blood that trailed from his nostrils had been cleaned up. He was transferred to a side ward of the Acute Admissions Unit and ventilated and monitored by an electrocardiograph. He was still guarded because that was a protocol (he was still technically alive) although the clinical staff considered it to be a meaningless act of state intransigence. The warder sat outside the room, bored and inattentive of the clinical staff who periodically went into the room, remained for perhaps ten minutes and then exited.

Marsham remained alive until just after four o'clock in the morning; Sulston had attended shortly before, summoning a porter to prep a gurney for quick transfer to the operating theatre so that Marsham's organs could be harvested.

Marsham's death was announced by the cardiac monitor; the clinical staff hurried in past the prison officer who was on duty outside the room. He stood as they rushed into the room and followed them, his tabloid newspaper with its half-done crossword puzzle on the floor by the orange plastic chair on which he had been sitting.

As it turned out, Marsham's widow forbad all use of his organs for transplant, and there was nothing that anyone could say to persuade her otherwise. She couldn't, however, prevent the coroner from ordering a post-mortem examination of his body; an inquest was opened and then adjourned for reports.

When Claire Woodforde heard that he had died, she frowned and said, "Odd, I thought he'd last longer than that."

She was going off duty, but she couldn't get the case out of her head. She reached home at half past seven to find her husband, still in his dressing gown and pyjamas, cooking breakfast; she didn't feel like bacon, eggs and tomatoes, but she wasn't cruel enough to stick to the truth. She ate the meal with him and told him how nice it was and how good it was of him to have cooked it. Matthew smiled, and perhaps he believed her, perhaps he didn't want to show that he didn't. In any case, he got up from the table and hugged her. He left the room to shower and dress for his day, also leaving her with the washing up of the breakfast things. She would do it later.

She sat and thought about the death of Edward Marsham, unable to calm her fears about it.

Chapter Two

"There's something that stinks about this, John."

Eisenmenger looked at her; he heard what she said, but he looked at her, too. Looking at Beverley Wharton had always been a mistake for him. He looked at Sergeant Bayes. That was a mistake, too, because he was young and good-looking and Eisenmenger imagined that, despite the age difference, Bayes and Beverley (how it tripped off the tongue!) were likely bedfellows. And that made him at once both jealous and regretful. He had once been her bedfellow, had held her and made her croon; and he, the fool that he was, had ended it.

"It sounds fairly straightforward to me."

He couldn't understand why he had accepted her invitation to meet . . .

Yes, he could . . .

He didn't want to, but he most certainly could understand.

He was cursed with a degree of insight that was at

times almost crippling. As it was now. He loved her still. Try as hard as he might, he couldn't persuade himself otherwise . . .

It was a pub that he knew well. She knew it well also. She knew it because he had introduced her to it. Was she playing mind tricks on him? No, scrap that. She was playing mind tricks on him, but was she doing it deliberately? That was the real question to ask. You have to know the right question to ask. All the greats – Newton, Einstein, Bohr – had known which question to pose, and only then gone looking for the answers.

"That's what everybody said. I say differently."

Bayes was young, but not too young. He was fairly handsome, as far as Eisenmenger could tell; perhaps a bit bulky, but that wouldn't be a problem for ten years until the muscle turned to fat. And a suspicion of the early signs of male pattern baldness, he judged. Or was he just being spiteful?

He said, "To which the immediate riposte must be 'Why do you say differently?' And you don't seem able to tell me."

He watched as Beverley looked around. She was drinking a white wine spritzer that he had bought her – Sauvignon Blanc (preferably from the Marlborough region of New Zealand) and sparkling water, not lemonade. Bayes, bless him, was drinking apple juice. Eisenmenger suspected that it was not made directly from crushed and filtered apples but Eisenmenger also suspected that the subtle niceties of

6

such things were of no concern to Sergeant Bayes. He, himself, was drinking ale: he had nothing to do that afternoon nor, indeed, most afternoons.

He continued, "Marsham was on remand for suspected child abuse. He was supposedly on suicide watch, although I doubt that it was a regime that was being strictly adhered to, since he still manages to unpick the stitching at the top of his shirt sleeves and make a short but effective noose. He hangs himself from the door hinge – God knows how – and has been unconscious and deprived of oxygen long enough to cause massive brain damage by the time he is discovered."

Her gaze returned to him, and he could see nothing within it that suggested warmth. *Perhaps that was because there was no warmth for him within her, he could hardly blame her. Would that it were otherwise . . .*

She smiled. He discovered that he had missed that smile.

He went on, "It is no surprise that Marsham died; it was inevitable."

"I know that," she replied.

"So why the interest?"

She said, "If you do the second autopsy as I want, perhaps you'll find out, John."

"The Royal College consider me to have retired," he pointed out. "They won't be happy . . ."

"Fuck the Royal College. If I want you to conduct a post-mortem examination, then you can do one and they can choke on their vintage port for all I care."

She sipped her drink. Bayes chugged his. Eisenmenger opted for a large mouthful of his ale, somewhere between the two. He sighed and then said thoughtfully, "How much?"

Bayes asked, "How much what?"

Beverley said, "A thousand?"

"How about fifteen hundred?"

"How about it?"

"I'll do it for fifteen hundred pounds."

"Why not do it for twelve hundred?"

Bayes looked on in silence; he was fidgeting, and Eisenmenger saw dissatisfaction in his body language. He took pleasure in this observation. He said just, "Okay."

She laughed, "That was too easy."

He smiled at her laugh. "I'd have done it for a thousand."

She was shaking her head as she stood; Eisenmenger reflected that it was typical of her to leave her glass half full. Bayes stood as well; his glass was empty except for three ice cubes. "When can you do it?" she asked.

"Anytime, now I'm not working regular hours."

"Tomorrow?"

"If you can make the arrangements with the mortuary."

"Tomorrow it is then."

"And you won't tell me what I'm supposed to be looking for? Why you think there's something fishy about this?"

"Nope."

She walked away, and Bayes hurried after her.

*

Outside, there was an odour of Indian cuisine from some-where and it was starting to rain. As they walked to the car, Bayes asked, "What did he mean? *Not working regular hours.*"

"He lucked into some sort of advisory job for an American TV company that's producing a forensic pathology drama, and then he got to co-author a spin-off novelisation that's doing pretty well. He doesn't need a day job."

They walked on, but she could tell that something was still bothering him. Eventually he asked, "Why are we bothering with this?"

She stopped abruptly. "Why are we bothering with this, *sir . . .*"

He bowed his head briefly. ". . . sir."

She looked at him. "Because *I* can smell something wrong about this, Sergeant, even if you can't."

"Nothing to do with that lunatic woman who's been pestering you?"

"That lunatic woman? You mean Claire Woodforde?"

"Nothing to do with her, then?"

"Something to do with her, yes, since you ask. Maybe she is lunatic, but there's something about Marsham's death I want properly investigated."

"He was a child abuser."

"It never got to trial, Bayes, so he was an innocent man. And even if it had, and he had been proved an abuser, his death still deserves to be properly investigated. Always remember that, Sergeant."

They began walking again. He asked, "Where are you going to get twelve hundred quid from?"

"I haven't the faintest idea, Sergeant."

"But . . ."

She turned on him. "If I don't give a fuck, why should you?"

"The new superintendent might not like . . ."

"The new superintendent can . . ." But she couldn't finish the sentiment, and let Bayes imagine for himself what the new superintendent could do. There was a pause whilst they stared at each other, two canines challenging one another, two combatants. He dropped his gaze before she did. She said tersely, "You have a lot to learn about working with me, Sergeant."

She walked on. He stared at her retreating form. His expression was hostile and hurt.

*

Inside the pub, Eisenmenger finished his pint and thought about ordering another. He decided that it was a good idea and went to the bar. Having sat back down, he examined the condensation that was forming on the curvature of the glass. He felt intrigued by his recent re-encounter with Beverley (re-encounter? Was there such a word?) and examined this emotion. Did it come merely from lust for her? Or did its origin lie at least partly in interest in the puzzle she had brought? Did the distinction matter? Had she brought a puzzle at all? His agreement to the bargain meant that he would win.

He would win because he was once more in contact with Beverley Wharton.

He would win because he trusted Beverley Wharton's instincts.

He would win because he would again be performing a post-mortem examination.

But he would lose, also.

He would lose because he couldn't escape the feeling that every case led him a little closer to his own death.

Chapter Three

"It says here that the first autopsy was done by Doctor C Sydenham." Eisenmenger had both the medical notes and the autopsy report on the table before him.

"That's right."

"*Charles* Sydenham?"

"That's him."

"Is he still going? He hasn't retired?"

"No."

"He must be in his seventies."

"I suppose."

Eisenmenger had always tried to make conversation with the technicians in whichever mortuary his work had taken him to, to butter them up, because it was important to have them on his side, especially when doing a second autopsy, when so much was contingent upon what the first autopsy had found. The technician who had assisted at that first post-mortem examination frequently had observations that were invaluable.

Perhaps not in this case, though.

At first Eisenmenger had thought Neil White was stupid; at second, he had thought him obstructive; at third, he had decided that his first impression had been correct. "You assisted Doctor Sydenham?" he said as they sat in the small office together, Sydenham's report on the desk in front of him.

Neil White nodded. He had a round face and small eyes that sheltered beneath a large brow; his hair was thinning. It was difficult not to think of him as anything other than stupid.

"How long did he take to do the autopsy?" he asked.

"An hour."

"An hour? Is that all?"

"He still paid me full whack." The tone was full of meaning.

"I'm sure. But he only took an hour?"

White nodded and there was a degree of implacability about him. It was of no import to him how long a pathologist took, but Eisenmenger felt differently. A full forensic post-mortem should have taken three or four hours. He had anticipated his would take less time because the dissection had already been done, but that was before discovering that Sydenham hadn't bothered to do his job properly.

He stood up. "Come on. We need to get started."

"Why?"

Eisenmenger was standing, but White wasn't. He kept his voice light. "Because this may take a little longer than I anticipated."

*

The body of Edward Marsham was a husk in which there was a white plastic bag; and in that bag were his organs. After White had undone his own stitching (it wasn't too bad, Eisenmenger noted), the bag was removed and transferred to a bench that ran along the side of the dissection room, beside a stainless steel sink. Eisenmenger undid the knot and upended the bag; the organs inside tumbled out in a wet, blood-soaked mess. He had expected to take a long time to separate the slices of liver, kidney, lung and brain, but it was relatively easy as Charles Sydenham had only put a single slice through each organ. He set about methodically putting many more slices through them, just to ensure that nothing of significance had been missed. Nothing had, but that didn't dissipate the feeling that Sydenham hadn't done a good job.

He turned his attention to the husk.

*

It was no surprise to Eisenmenger that the ligature marks around Marsham's neck were faint, or that there was no damage to the windpipe; only a rope left a deep mark, cloth such as Marsham had used never did. Marsham had died because his ligature had squeezed the vagus nerves in his neck and that, in turn, had slowed, possibly even stopped, his heart.

The backs of both hands were severely bruised and each bore a tiny puncture mark. Sydenham's report made brief mention of a plastic venous access point in the back of each hand. Eisenmenger asked of White, "Where are the venflons?"

White hesitated. "The venflons?" he asked, as if Eisenmenger had asked for pieces of a meteorite. Eisenmenger could almost see the defensive wall that he was erecting as he spoke.

"Yes. They were presumably still attached to the body when Charles started the autopsy. Where are they now?"

White frowned. "Why?"

Eisenmenger didn't think it was any of White's business and was beginning to suspect that they had been thrown away which, if so, was potentially a criminal act. Before he could summon a reply that was sufficiently withering, though, White left the dissection room. He returned a few moments later with two sealed plastic bags, each containing a bloodstained venflon. Both were labelled with Marsham's full name, the date of the autopsy and the hand from which they had been taken.

He handed them both to Eisenmenger who looked at them closely, then said, "I need to look at the notes again."

Chapter Four

"Tell me I'm right, John."

Beverley's eyes flicked to Bayes, who was out of earshot at the counter of the coffee shop. She hoped that he'd remember this time that she liked her coffee black and sugarless; working in a new sergeant was always hard going, but Bayes seemed to be proving more intransigent than most. Would she bed him, she wondered? Maybe she was getting too old for such behaviour. After her time with John Eisenmenger, sex no longer seemed such an easy escape; it merely took her from one place to another, and the place in which she arrived was not necessarily better than the one she had left. Since she had become a chief inspector, she no longer felt that urge to sleep with her superiors; that insecurity seemed to have evaporated. The corollary seemed to be to ask herself why sleep with her juniors unless she wanted to?

"I don't know, Beverley. I can't prove you right . . ."

She held the phone more tightly to her ear, despite herself. "But you can't totally exclude it?"

"Of course, I can't."

His voice was soft; always had been. Even down a phone line. She had always liked it, for a while she had loved it; at this moment, she thought it was the most wonderful thing in her universe. "You do?"

"I've found something . . . odd."

"Go on."

But Eisenmenger was never one to be straightforward. "Is the toxicology report back?"

"Later today."

"Let's meet when you've got it."

"Where?"

"At the mortuary."

With which he cut the connection.

*

The toxicology report on the samples taken from Marsham by Charles Sydenham contained nothing of interest, as far as both Bayes and Beverley could see. When Eisenmenger arrived in the mortuary, it was after five p.m., and Bayes and Beverley were already there, seated in the office. White was there, as well, clearly unhappy to be kept at work comparatively late. When Beverley handed Eisenmenger the toxicology report, he read it eagerly, watched by all three of them, but did not seem much discontented by it.

He handed it back to Beverley. White's eyes stayed on him, full of hostility. Despite the fact that Eisenmenger had given him a hefty gratuity after the autopsy, he was still not a happy man.

"Well?" she asked. "It's negative."

"So I see." He sounded pleased.

"Is that good?"

"It's not bad."

"What the fuck does that mean?" enquired Bayes. Eisenmenger was thinking deeply; it was a familiar pose to Beverley, alien to Bayes.

"You said that you'd discovered something, John," she reminded him. "What was it?"

Without a further word, he left the office. They heard the sound of a fridge door opening and then being slammed shut. White almost stood up; his expression was deeply concerned. Eisenmenger's return to the office was immediate. He had with him the two venflons still in their bags. He handed them over to Beverley, who looked at them, then handed them to Bayes. She turned back to Eisenmenger. "What of them?"

"One contains blood, the other doesn't."

Bayes said, "So?" His tone suggested that something close to contempt was in his mind.

"Marsham had a drip inserted into each of these; one was normal saline, the other five per cent dextrose."

"So?" repeated Bayes. He sounded bored.

"When a bag of intravenous fluid empties, blood can

18

backtrack into the plastic tube, but neither bag was empty when Marsham died."

Beverley took the bags back from Bayes. "So how did blood get into this one?" she asked.

"I was wondering if someone injected something into Marsham, and then sucked back some blood to ensure that there would be no trace of it left in the venflon."

"But the toxicology's come back negative," pointed out Bayes.

"Some things aren't detected by a forensic laboratory analysis."

"Such as what?"

Eisenmenger shrugged. "The one that springs instantly to mind is potassium chloride. A bolus injected into the circulation may well cause a fatal heart dysrhythmia." He looked around, to blank looks and added, "The heart would misfire."

"And be undetectable at autopsy?"

"Under these circumstances, yes."

He looked around. White looked no less irritated; Bayes looked sceptical; even Beverley's face betrayed disappointment.

Bayes shook his young, handsome head. White was saying nothing, but was looking on with interest. Bayes demanded, "Why can't we just ask them to measure the level of potassium chloride?"

"Because the blood levels of potassium rise very quickly after death in all bodies. It's because, although there isn't a lot in the blood in life, there's a huge amount inside the cells. Very quickly after death it leaks out and the blood levels rise, swamping anything that might be injected just prior to the end of life."

"So you're postulating that he was killed by a means that we can't detect. And all from the observation that one of these . . ." Bayes waved a hand at the bags that were now on the table in front of Beverley, ". . . has blood in?" His voice carried so much mockery it was curling his upper lip.

"It's a possibility." Eisenmenger behaved characteristically in his non-committal reply, although he didn't bend before Bayes' disdain.

Bayes made a sound that came from the back of his throat, his expression reinforcing the problems he clearly had with this hypothesis. Beverley asked, "How quickly would a bolus such as you describe cause the heart to misfire?"

Bayes looked at her and obviously thought she was mad even to entertain Eisenmenger's ludicrous idea.

"Just a few seconds."

She nodded, as if he had only confirmed what she had suspected all along. Bayes said, "What we seem to be overlooking is that this man was going to die anyway. In which case, why bother?"

Eisenmenger replied slowly, "I can't answer that."

Bayes turned to his superior. "Can you?"

She returned his gaze slowly. "Can you . . . *sir*."

They stared at each other; inevitably, he backed down. "Can you, sir?"

She smiled sweetly. "Let's see."

Chapter Five

"I'm sorry to bother you."

"Not at all." Eisenmenger didn't know Claire Woodforde personally, although he had heard the name. He couldn't help but hold intensivists in some awe, although the logical part of his mind told him that they were in effect no different from any other doctor, including pathologists. There was a glamour to their role, though, that could not be dissipated by logic alone. After all, they kept people alive who were severely ill; often they actually made them better. People who shouldn't have done, lived again. That was something he and his kind had never achieved.

And her voice on the phone was deep and somehow inviting . . .

"Could we meet up, do you think?"

He hesitated, partly because he *always* hesitated, and partly because he genuinely couldn't think why they should.

Accordingly, he asked, "Why?" and then quickly, "I'm sorry if that sounded rude."

She laughed. "It's a fair question."

He waited.

"Because a little bird told me that you performed a second autopsy on Edward Marsham, and you thought he might have been murdered."

"That's not precisely what I concluded . . ."

"So you say he definitely wasn't murdered?"

He thought of the venflons. "I didn't say that either," he admitted.

"Well, then. I think we should talk to each other."

"Are you saying you've got evidence that might sway my opinion?"

"I'll explain face to face."

They arranged to meet in the hospital coffee shop at eight o'clock the next morning. After he had put down the phone, Eisenmenger speculated who that "little bird" might be, surmising that it had been Neil White. He then speculated why his hypothesis should matter to Claire Woodforde; he had no answer for that one, though.

Bayes wouldn't leave it alone. "We've got too much to do without bothering about this."

"'This' being?"

They were in her office, their desks at right angles, his facing the door, hers to the left of the window. The weather was blowy outside, ruffling the bright green leaves of spring on the trees and bushes. The daffodils, now in full bloom, bent to a force that was beyond them; she wished that it was within her nature to be so compliant. Bayes' words brought her back and the thought was gone. It wasn't within her nature to bend with the winds that blew through her life; the stronger the gale, the more she resisted. "The death of Marsham."

"Why?" she was genuinely interested, even as her internal thermostat registered rising irritation. She could have guessed his next words, could have written them on a sheet of paper and put them in a white envelope to produce later like a cheap magician.

"For one thing, he was a piece of shit who had abused his step-daughter."

"He was on remand, Sergeant. We've discussed this, if you recall. Nothing had been proved, and might never have been proved."

"Or it might have been."

She held her breath, counting to ten, trying to retain her temper; he looked at her. She said eventually and as lightly as she could, "We'll never know, will we?"

"No."

"In the eyes of the law, he remains innocent."

"Begging the question, why did he hang himself?"

"Something else we'll never know." She smiled tightly at him, which infuriated him.

He said, "You still can't explain why anyone should kill him."

"No, I can't."

"Well, then . . ." He was triumphant.

"It doesn't matter a fuck that I can't think of a reason why. Lots of times I start off not knowing why a murder occurs. Can you see that?" She was being as patient as she could be, telling herself that he was new to the work.

"I suppose so."

"The fact that neither of us can think of a reason why a man who was going to die very shortly should be murdered is neither here nor there."

He didn't say anything, which she thought might be a good thing. She added, "We're all going to die, Bayes, and we've all done things we're ashamed of, but that doesn't mean we as police officers should pick and choose who's worthy of life and who isn't."

She thought she had persuaded him.

She thought wrong.

"We don't definitely know that he was murdered, though. We only have Eisenmenger's word for it, and even he's not saying so for certain."

She opened her mouth but he got there first. He was leaning forward in his chair, a cheap plastic pen grasped in both hands; he examined it as he spoke. "And I know about John Eisenmenger."

"You do?"

"Something of a difficult person but he has a knack for being right. Not infallible, but occasionally brilliant."

Again, she opened her mouth and again he spoke before she could. "And I know about your . . . *history*."

Is that what it was? What it is? History? Like the kings and queens of Great Britain? And that tone! Was it disgust? Or was it conceivably something else? Something more dangerous to her?

She stood up and he looked at her. She was pleased to see something that might have been fear in his eyes. He'd overstepped the mark and he knew it. She walked around her desk and towards his, coming to stand beside its left-hand side. She wore blue jeans, a white tee and a black leather jacket; on the nails of each finger of each hand was Crimson Peak. The hands curled around the edges of the grey desk. She leaned towards him on straight arms, her face one of open, frank hostility. "That has nothing to do with you, Bayes. Understand?"

He nodded slowly. She straightened up. He said, "There's still nothing that demands our attention . . . sir."

She looked down upon him, unable to decide about this man before her. She could understand his attitude to the case, she supposed. She had had salad days once . . . But there was something about him, something that worried her. She said, "The prison officer who was on duty outside Marsham's room . . ."

"Jerry Wickham?" She noted that he recalled the name immediately and was impressed, but she didn't let it show.

"He runs a website."

He said nothing.

She continued, "It's called 'Savetheinnocents'. All one word. Look it up."

As he was doing so, she said, "He started it last September

when his niece killed herself aged fifteen. Her last posting on Facebook talked about the abuse she had suffered from her stepfather since she was six."

Bayes was staring at the website.

Beverley said, "There was an incident last August in which a suspected paedophile's house was burned down. Wickham lives nearby. He was questioned but released because there was no evidence to connect him with the crime."

"And you think he might have killed Marsham?" She said nothing as she returned to her desk. "But I still come back to why? Marsham was dying. He didn't need to do anything."

"And I still come back to the fact that Marsham's inevitable demise doesn't necessarily mean someone didn't feel the need to murder him anyway. Wickham fits the bill admirably." She indicated his computer screen. "If you spend long enough with that website, you'll see that Wickham's a driven man."

"So driven that he couldn't wait a few hours for nature to take its course?"

"Maybe."

She saw that he was unconvinced. Nor was she, in truth. She just couldn't see Wickham as the killer. That didn't mean, though, that her antennae weren't twitching even if she couldn't work out why.

"And where would he get a solution of potassium? And would he know how to inject it?"

She found it hard not to like him, not least because he was bright and was asking very pertinent questions. She was damned if she was going to let him know any of this, though. She said, "His wife works as a teaching assistant in a large secondary school. I could envisage that she wouldn't find it too difficult to get hold of some potassium chloride. The syringe and the needle wouldn't be too much of an insurmountable problem for a prison warder."

With which she saw with no little pleasure that she had stumped him. He thought about what she had just said. "I still say, it's not as important as some of the other cases we've got."

Choose your battles.

Perhaps, when younger, she should have done that. Now that the years had flowed past her, it seemed like lunacy to ignore such advice. Her temper, though, wasn't interested. "Listen, Sergeant," it said and she was shocked to hear the words coming from her mouth, and feel the adrenaline surge within her, and to notice that she was leaning forward in her chair. "*I'll* decide what we investigate and when."

He stared at her, openly hostile, for a moment before taking a deep breath. "What would you like to do, sir?"

"We go and talk to Mr Wickham . . . as a witness. Nothing more."

Chapter Six

"Thanks for meeting me."

She was tall, with bobbed hair that was blonde; was that her natural colour? He could never tell. She had a lightly snubbed nose and pale blue eyes that pierced him. She radiated intelligence.

"I have half an hour," she continued and then grimaced. "What do you have to do at eight-thirty?"

"Just an ENT list. Grommets, mostly."

"Exciting," he said drily.

She laughed. It was a nice sound, he decided. "That's anaesthetics for you. You hope and pray that nothing will gino wrong, but you also desperately want something to happen to alleviate the boredom."

"Boring is good for the patient but not for you?"

"It's part of the reason I went into intensive care."

At that time of the morning, there were few patients as

they sat in the coffee shop; the only people around them were nurses who had just come off duty, porters and cleaners, and the inevitable subsection of anonymous types in smart business clothes – perhaps hospital managers, perhaps reps from companies that were trying to sell things to somebody. She had on aubergine scrubs, and no ring he noted. Not that that meant anything.

"What can I do for you?" he asked.

She looked around. It *was* dark in there, he thought. A typical commercial coffee shop, with its confectioneries, sandwiches and drinks under bright lights, its Easter specials – cupcakes with small blue speckled eggs on top, slices of Simnel cake and Easter eggs – especially prominent, whilst the rest of the place was in sub-crepuscular gloom. She leaned forward. "What I was told was pretty garbled . . ."

"Would you be talking about Neil White?"

She looked startled and, perhaps for just a moment, she was about to lie but she said, "Yes." She dropped her head as if ashamed of this admission and he wondered why. "He said that you thought Marsham might have been murdered."

"It's a possibility. Nothing more."

She leaned back in her chair, her hands cradling the flat white that he had bought her. She said quietly, "I believe it."

"Why?"

"Because I think that a murderer's been operating in this hospital for a long time."

His cappuccino halted on its way to his lips. He put it back down untasted, then thought about what she had just said. Eventually he asked, "Tell me why you were speaking to Neil White."

"What?"

He smiled. "Forgive me. My mind works in odd ways. You're a consultant anaesthetist and intensivist. He's the mortuary manager. Why would he be talking to you?"

"I was in the mortuary completing a cremation document. We were just gossiping."

He thought about this reply, trying to determine if it were true, or perhaps how much truth there was in it. There was *some* truth, he could tell; but was it *all* true, and was it the *whole* truth? He nodded and smiled. "What makes you think that this . . . death is just the latest of a series of murders?"

She drained her cup. "We've been in special measures for two, long years now."

"I know."

"Among the many problems that the CQC identified was a high mortality rate."

"So?"

"The trust knew that it had been creeping up, of course . . ."

"So I would hope."

"And that it was due mainly to post-operative deaths."

"Okay . . ."

"But no one could see a pattern to it beyond that observation. It wasn't consistently colorectal patients, or ENT, or gynae, or anything."

"So it wasn't due to a particular surgeon or department."

"No."

She found the next few words difficult. "And then it spiked a couple of years ago and it's remained high ever since. I suggested that it might be a nurse over a year ago, but I was told in no uncertain terms not to repeat that suggestion without a lot more proof than I had."

"By whom?"

A smile tripped across her lips and he wondered about that; it surely wasn't because of his use of the objective case? She said, "The chief operating officer, Mr Greeley."

"Didn't want a scandal?"

"No."

"Unfortunately, I haven't got proof either, Doctor Woodforde. Like you, it's little more than speculation."

"Claire, please."

"And I'm John."

They didn't shake hands except in a virtual sense.

She looked at her watch. "I really need to get to theatres." She stood. "Thanks for the coffee."

He watched her go without saying another word; his head was full of them, though.

Chapter Seven

It had been easy to gain access to Wickham's rota from the prison and so they knew that he would be at home when they called. They had to ring the doorbell three times before receiving a response, but they were persistent. The response, though, wasn't entirely to their liking.

The door opened and confronting Bayes was a small, angry, grey-haired woman. She had high cheekbones below eyes that were yellowed but still sharp. She was dressed in a housecoat that did nothing for the sergeant, although Beverley was immediately transported to her youth when such apparel was all the rage. Everyone wore housecoats when she had been young; certainly, her mother had done. It was a false memory, though, she knew; it had been filtered and moulded and sculpted, so that it was as perfect as Michelangelo's *David*, and equally unrepresentative of truth.

She seemed unconcerned by the badge that Bayes held

up to her face, her eyes preferring to focus on Beverley. "Yes?" Her tone was disparaging, contemptuous.

"We'd like to talk to Jerry," said Bayes.

"He's asleep. He's on nights."

It was nearly five o'clock in the afternoon. They had deliberately waited until that time because they had known that he was working nights that week, and assumed that he would be up by then. Despite the deflection, Bayes persevered. "We know. Wake him, please."

She began to argue but they had woken the sleeping beast. "Who is it, Jean?" floated down the stairs and wafted past the woman in the housecoat. The voice came from sleep; it was deep and seemed anchored in something sticky. It was deep, too.

Jean and Jerry. Like an American sitcom from the seventies, thought Beverley. It could have been Fred Flintstone up there.

She called back, "It's the police." Her look back to Bayes and Beverley was venomous. Then back to her husband, "They want to speak to you."

The pause was long before, "Okay . . ." Beverley thought that it sounded resigned, and wondered, *Resigned to what?* Jean Wickham looked as if she had taken a bite out of a fruit, expecting it to be an orange and finding it to be a lemon, but she stood aside, saying, "You'd best come in."

In the front room of the small terraced house, Beverley sat, although the cheap armchair was uncomfortable. Bayes remained standing. Mrs Wickham didn't offer them refreshment as they waited; she didn't even grace them with her presence. The traffic outside the house was continual but not continuous, which made it all the more irritating, especially as the secondary glazing – that had been rather shoddily installed, Bayes noted – didn't do much to reduce the sound.

It took nearly fifteen minutes for Wickham to arrive and, even then he was still in his night attire. Beverley wondered what he had been doing in the time they had been waiting. She could only conclude that it had been a deliberate ploy, presumably to show his indifference. She didn't mind; she had met this attitude before. It never lasted.

Bayes asked, "What kept you?" She had the impression that he, too, knew exactly what Jerry Wickham had been playing at.

Wickham was a large man, an ideal prison officer. He was over fifty and running to fat; his breathing was heavy. He didn't like the way that Bayes addressed him apparently, for he faced up to him. Bayes, at nearly two metres tall and giving Wickham twenty years, wasn't particularly concerned. Indeed, Beverley thought that he gave every indication that he would quite enjoy a scrap with him.

theabout the death of Edward Marsham."

He turned to her, "Marsham?"

"If you wouldn't mind."

"Why?"

She had known that he would ask this and her prevarication was rehearsed. "We're just following protocol, Mr

Wickham. There's no implication in our talking to you. No assumptions are being made."

"I should fucking well hope not." He sat down heavily in another armchair. "The bastard was dying. I was only outside his room as a formality."

"Bastard?" asked Bayes, who had produced a notebook that he now looked up from.

"Figure of speech." Beverley glanced warningly at Bayes who apparently didn't notice; Wickham did, though. He smiled nastily. "I am what I am."

Bayes sneered. "A bigot?"

Wickham laughed. "Maybe. What's wrong with that, if I am?"

Beverley said, "Nobody's accusing you of anything, Mr Wickham."

"I didn't kill him, but I'm not sorry the cunt's dead."

She sighed. "We just came here to talk to you, Mr Wickham, because he decided to hang himself when he was in prison, which makes it our business to investigate, and because you were outside the room when he died. No other reason."

He looked at Bayes. "Really?"

"Really."

He thought about this, then took a deep breath. "Okay."

She glared at Bayes; it was designed to tell him to shut up, but he wasn't looking at her. She said, "We appreciate that Marsham had been diagnosed as brain dead and he was therefore going to die sooner rather than later, but there must have been a lot of activity going in and out of his room."

He snorted. "You can say that again."

"Can you tell us who?"

"They mostly wore those tunic things."

"Scrubs?"

"Aye, scrubs. Different colours. Don't know what that means."

Bayes asked, "Can you tell us what colours?"

Wickham frowned. "Why?"

Beverley thought it a good question. If the fat prison warder hadn't asked it, then she might well have done, albeit after they had taken their leave.

"Just try to remember what the colours were, Mr Wickham."

He wrinkled his nose as if he could smell flatus. "Blue, I think. Light blue and dark blue. And dark green, and a sort of mauvey colour."

"But you couldn't say who they were. Whether they were nurses, doctors, or something else?" Beverley tried to get a sense of direction back in the interrogation.

"Nope." He seemed very satisfied with his ignorance and couldn't see why she was stressing about it.

"Who was last in?"

"What?"

"Who was last in before he died?"

He shrugged. "How am I supposed . . .?" He stopped. "You *do* think he was killed."

Bayes weighed in again. "Just answer the question." In Beverley's opinion, every intervention from her sergeant was made in hobnailed boots with steel toecaps, and she didn't think it was always necessary to jump on a witness's head, even if that witness could conceivably be a perpetrator.

Wickham stared at Bayes, and Beverley thought for a moment that the interjection would prove counterproductive, but he frowned with the effort of concentration and said eventually, "I think it was the doctor who said he was going to die."

Bayes asked immediately, "Woodforde?"

"If you say so."

"A woman, right?"

"Yeah . . ."

On their way out, Bayes said to Jean Wickham, "You work as a teaching assistant. Is that right?"

She was at once suspicious and defensive. "What of it?" Jerry Wickham paused on his way upstairs.

"Where?"

She gestured with her grey hair. "Community school up the road."

"What ages?"

"All of 'em."

"What subjects do you help out with?"

She had reached the limit of her compliance. Wickham had been on his way back upstairs but now he came back down a couple of stairs. "Why are you interrogating my wife?" he demanded.

Beverley had been standing by the front door. She came back to support Bayes; she wasn't entirely sure why he had decided to confront Jean Wickham, but she instinctively moved to stand beside him. She said, "Just answer the question, Mrs Wickham."

She glanced at her husband. "Wherever I'm wanted."

"Including the science labs?"

"On occasion."

Bayes looked at Beverley. Beverley looked at Jerry Wickham. His expression was unreadable.

Chapter Eight

Eisenmenger had woken with a headache that wouldn't go. He had taken paracetamol first thing with a cup of tea and then ibuprofen with a piece of toast and olive oil spread, and was waiting for something, anything, to have an effect. He stared out of the window watching nothing in particular, finding little interest in any of it. His house was in a mews and very quiet. When he had found the house, he had been delighted. Now, in profound boredom, he regretted it. The phone rang.

"Hello?"

"Doctor Eisenmenger?"

"Speaking."

"The name's Greeley. Andrew Greeley."

Was that supposed to mean something to him? It did, vaguely. "Yes?"

"I work at the infirmary. I was wondering if you could find time for a chat . . ."

Greeley plus infirmary . . . Something rang at the back of his head, and perhaps it was a bell, but it was rather discordant. The bell could have been cracked, but it could easily have been a hammer dropped on a tin tray. He said cautiously, "What about?"

There was a hesitation. "I understand that you did an autopsy on Edward Marsham."

"What of it?"

"I'd like to discuss your results."

"Why would they be of interest to you?" Rude, he knew, but he didn't know how, or care, to phrase it otherwise.

"I'm the chief operating officer of the trust, and you're telling everyone that a patient might have been murdered in my hospital. That's why."

*

Greeley's office was inside the Trust Headquarters, which were located at the back of the infirmary. Eisenmenger found it eventually, but only with some difficulty, not least because of the intercom to get into the building, which didn't work properly. After shouting into the stainless steel box, there was a tinny buzz that might have been a human being asking a question, although he couldn't be sure. He shouted again. The same tinny voice. He might have been there a long time more had someone not come up behind him, smiled and said, "I do wish someone would replace that bloody thing."

Eisenmenger straightened and turned. The stranger was

short but not fat. He had sandy hair and bright blue eyes. He asked, "Do you have an appointment with someone?"

"Mr Greeley's expecting me."

He nodded and smiled, then punched a number in on the keypad below the grill that Eisenmenger had been shouting into. There was a buzz and he pushed the door open with his hand. "After you," he said. "Reception's to your right."

He walked rapidly to the left.

Eisenmenger did as directed and, from reception, was escorted to Greeley's office, aware that he was following in the footsteps of the short man. The receptionist knocked on the door.

"Yes? Come in."

The receptionist complied with the command. "Doctor Eisenmenger to see you."

Eisenmenger entered, finding two men present, one of them the man who had admitted him. The other stood, holding out his hand. "Thank you for coming. Please, sit down."

The office was small and decorated in a nauseous shade of yellow. There was a small, round wooden table at which the two men were sitting, with two more wooden chairs opposite. The only other furniture in the room was a corner desk under which a more conventional office chair snuggled. The carpet was clean. On the walls were abstract prints that left Eisenmenger cold. The view from the window over the desk was of a railway line. Eisenmenger wondered why the bushes along railway tracks were always so grubby; the rain only made them greasy and grimy.

"Coffee?" asked the receptionist.

It was the shorter man who responded. "Yes, please, Julie."

Julie left them as Eisenmenger sat. The shorter man smiled. "My name's Gary Benson. I'm the CEO of the trust." He proffered a hand that Eisenmenger took; his handshake was weak and moist, the kind that made Eisenmenger want to wipe his hand on something. "And this is Andrew, whom you've already talked to on the phone."

Greeley was thin to the point of asceticism; his skin looked dry and was pallid, as if he were sickening for something. He spoke through his nose, one that he peered down as if pronouncing judgement. Eisenmenger wondered if he had some sort of eye muscle palsy. He said, "Two of you. That seems less like 'a chat', more like a 'telling off'."

"Not at all." Benson mocked such an idea. "It wasn't planned that I should be here. I just had a spare half an hour . . ." Eisenmenger didn't believe that any more than Benson or Greeley did, but said nothing to contradict it.

Choose your battles . . .

Besides, he was intrigued that the chief executive and chief operating officer – the two most important executives in the trust – should find enough time to attend this meeting. His thoughts on the death of Edward Marsham seemed to have pressed a few buttons . . .

Julie returned with a large cafetière and four mugs, each bearing the pale blue NHS logo; they were heavy and definitely not bone china. After they had sorted who had milk, and who had sugar, Greeley began. "I understand that you were asked to do a second autopsy on Mr Marsham."

"By the police, yes."

He nodded weakly, as if this were true but unimportant, to him at least. "And that you found that he had been murdered."

"No."

He was surprised. So was Gary Benson, Eisenmenger noted.

"No?"

"I merely said that it was a possibility. He died earlier than expected, after all."

"But you agree he *was* dying?"

"Oh, absolutely."

The two men opposite him looked at each other. Benson spoke. "We have over two hundred consultants working for this trust." Eisenmenger didn't know how to receive this fascinating datum and said nothing. Benson leaned forward, "Why, we have over thirty consultant anaesthetists alone."

"It's odd how they multiply." Eisenmenger's tone was laden with irony. "You only have to look away and, when you turn back, there's another one. Perhaps it's mitosis rather than meiosis."

Benson didn't appreciate the flippancy; Eisenmenger

suspected that he didn't understand it. The chief executive said, "It's inevitable that amongst so many, one or two prove . . . *problematic.*"

Eisenmenger sighed. "Doctor Woodforde?" he guessed.

"She's been quite a pain with her wild theories . . ." This from Greeley.

"About a mass murderer loose in the hospital?"

". . . We've investigated the excess mortality in this trust thoroughly; so have independent bodies such as the CQC and NHS Improvement. There's nothing to her insinuations."

"But there *is* an excess of deaths here?"

Greeley looked at Benson. Benson said, "Yes. As there is in many trusts, where there is no suggestion that a mass murderer is on the loose."

Benson chimed in, "Which makes your hypothesis about Mr Marsham somewhat unfortunate."

"It's strengthened her . . ." Greeley groped for the word. ". . . delusion that there is someone in this hospital who is going around killing patients."

Eisenmenger sipped his coffee. It wasn't too bad, he thought. Certainly better than the stuff he remembered from countless lunchtime clinical meetings, when it had come from a heated metal urn and had an excess of chicory and had enjoyed only a fleeting relationship with a coffee bean. He guessed that Trust HQ didn't rely on the same source. "I merely said it was a possibility that I couldn't, from the autopsy findings, totally exclude." Greeley would have spoken then, but he rode over him. "And I said so in a confidential report."

Benson showed his relief. "I see."

"Which makes me wonder how the trust got hold of it."

Benson and Greeley did their thing with the looks again. It occurred to Eisenmenger that perhaps the meeting wasn't going as they had expected. Benson said reassuringly, "We haven't had sight of the report, Doctor Eisenmenger."

"Really?"

"Oh, no." He shook his head vehemently. Greeley joined in. "So this is hearsay?"

"Well . . ." Benson looked as if he didn't know where the sentence was heading.

"I wouldn't put it quite that way," contributed the chief operating officer.

Eisenmenger put his half-full cup down. "Please put your minds at rest, gentlemen. I have no intention of joining Doctor Woodforde's crusade." He stood. "If that's all?"

Greeley looked at Benson, who was clearly the real power in the room, and who said now, "Thank you for coming, Doctor Eisenmenger . . ."

Greeley stood and proffered his hand. Rather belatedly, Benson did likewise. He said, "And if you're interested, we have one or two vacancies in the Histopathology Department . . .? I'm sure that if you were to make informal enquiries of them, we could come to some sort of arrangement that would be mutually agreeable."

The transition between Greeley's desiccated handshake

and Benson's sweaty paw was most disturbing. Eisenmenger murmured, "I'll bear it in mind, Mr Benson." They all knew that he was lying. He suspected that it hadn't been the first lie uttered in that room in the last fifteen minutes. Outside, as he walked back to the entrance to the building, he wiped his hand on his cords.

In the car park, he bumped into Claire Woodforde, and not coincidentally he quickly concluded. She behaved in a most peculiar manner, he now saw.

She said, having glanced over her shoulder at Trust HQ, "I'm glad I caught you."

"You are?"

"You were summoned to see Mr Greeley."

"Benson was there as well."

Her eyebrows rose up her face. "The CEO as well?"

He nodded. "How do you know?"

"I keep my ear to the ground . . ."

She had a mole in the secretariat, he guessed.

"It was about your autopsy findings, wasn't it?"

He didn't want to talk to her. He had a new perspective, one that her present manner seemed to chime with.

"It was confidential, Claire."

He walked on to his car. She followed. "They said I was . . . What? Wrong? Mad?"

He halted and turned to her. "'Deluded' was the word they used."

She laughed. It was a slightly lunatic sound to his ears at that moment. "Do you believe them?" she asked.

He looked directly at her. "Of course I don't believe that you have a delusion . . ." he began carefully.

"But you think I'm wrong? Like them?"

"I don't have enough information either way," he replied cautiously.

She looked again over her shoulder. It was the action of someone who was paranoid. He thought, *You're not helping yourself.*

She pressed a piece of paper into his hand. "This is my home address. Will you come to dinner? Tomorrow night? We can talk then."

Before he could decline, she had turned away and was hurrying across the car park, her head down as if she didn't want anyone in Trust HQ to see her. He looked at the paper, half expecting to see green ink, but her scrawl was in a reassuring blue. He debated throwing it away, but instead he thrust it into his pocket.

Chapter Nine

"The superintendent wants to see you."

Beverley had known that this day would come, but that didn't make the words any more welcome. The uniformed sergeant who had delivered this summons, was poking her head around the door of Beverley's office. Bayes' look across at Beverley was peculiar, she thought. She replied, "Okay."

"Now."

Her response was filled with anger. "Okay, Sergeant."

The head withdrew. Beverley transferred her glance to Bayes, who was still looking at her, now quizzically. "Yes?" she demanded.

Bayes shrugged but said nothing.

She continued what she was doing but couldn't escape the psychological pull of the summons. She stood up and went to the door without speaking to her sergeant. She walked along the corridor, up the two flights of stairs at the end, and back along the corridor. At the back of her mind she noted that Superintendent Lambert's office was almost directly above hers. *How ironic.*

She knocked on the door.

"Come." How typical of Lambert! Why use two syllables when one will suffice?

She entered his office. He looked up at once. She hadn't expected a welcoming smile and didn't get one. "Chief Inspector Wharton." Just that, nothing more, but the tone was hostile, just as it had always been.

Along with the accoutrements, promotion had brought a degree of flabbiness around his jowls, she thought. Still, the office was nice. Clean carpet, big desk, certificates on the walls; she had never been one for certificates on the walls, considering it to be affectation and the professional equivalent of buying a large, fast car as a form of penis substitute.

"Sir." She stood before his desk. He just stared at her for a moment. He was greyer, she noted, and looked out of condition. Such was age and she knew that she had not completely escaped similar effects.

"We find ourselves working together again." He might have been chewing metal polish spread on white bread without butter.

"Yes, sir."

"We have never liked each other."

"Sir . . ."

He shook his head. "Don't. It's a fact."

"Yes . . . sir." She hadn't been about to argue, but she let him think otherwise. Letting people think the wrong thing was a useful tactic, she had found.

"We are both promoted." He clearly thought that *his* promotion was reasonable, possibly even inevitable, whereas *hers* was more of a surprise to him. She had exactly the opposite opinion. "And with that comes more responsibility."

She said nothing.

He looked down at the surface of his desk. "I have here a list of your cases." She remained standing and silent. "You've been spending a deal of time on the death of Edward Marsham, I see." He looked up. His grey eyes were suddenly hostile. "Why?"

Did Bayes come bleating to you about it being a waste of time? "Sir, there was a question . . ."

"Yes, Doctor Eisenmenger's autopsy report." He had papers on his desk next to his keyboard. So much for the paperless office, she didn't say. He sighed. "You've always placed a lot of value on Eisenmenger, haven't you?"

"I suppose so."

He looked up at her, his eyebrows lowered as if he had heard impertinence in her reply. She hadn't meant to be in any way insubordinate. "Has it occurred to you that he's overrated?"

"To be fair, sir, John merely said that it was a possibility that Marsham's death was suspicious."

"John?"

"Doctor Eisenmenger."

He held his gaze upon her. What did he know about her relationship with John Eisenmenger? Probably everything, even though they hadn't worked together for a long time and he had only started in his present position the day before. "I understand Eisenmenger charged twelve hundred pounds."

"More or less the standard rate for a forensic autopsy fee."

"An unnecessary one. Charles Sydenham had already performed a post-mortem examination and found nothing untoward about the death."

"It depends on your point of view whether you consider a second post-mortem was unnecessary, sir."

"Well, Wharton, my point of view is that it was unnecessary to spend a further twelve hundred pounds on the death of Edward Marsham, only to be told that it is *possible* that someone hastened his death."

She thought about arguing, but only thought about it. In the event, she remained silent, reflecting that it was the better part of valour so to do. He picked up a pencil and struck through something on the list of her active cases. He looked up at her, "Waste no more time on it, Wharton. You've plenty of other things to worry about."

She left the office shortly afterwards, in no doubt that one of the things she had to worry about was inside the office behind her.

A Kiss Before Killing

Back in her office, she didn't have the chance to bollock Bayes because as soon as she walked in, he said excitedly, "A body's been uncovered in the city."

"Murder?"

"Oh, yes." He sounded disturbingly happy.

Chapter Ten

"Slow down."

"But . . ."

"It's a body, Bayes. It's not going anywhere."

"But time is of the *essence* at the start of a murder case."

Is that a quote? It certainly sounds like one.

"A few minutes won't make any difference; and if we're involved in a collision, that might slow us up considerably, especially if one of us ends up requiring hospitalisation or even an undertaker."

He slowed down to seventy miles an hour, the speed limit on the duel carriageway. She said after a few seconds, "Where were you before you transferred here?"

"Tewkesbury."

"Doing what?"

"Anything and everything."

She guessed that meant domestics, missing dogs, TWOCs

and low-level theft. Anything more important wouldn't have gone anywhere near a local police station. No wonder he was so excited to have a real body to deal with. "Are you with anyone?"

He took his eyes off the road to look across at her. "Pardon?"

"Are you with anyone? Do you have a 'significant other' as the current terminology would have it?"

He opened his mouth, snatched another sideways glance at her. "Well . . ." He sounded uncomfortable.

"I'm not coming onto you, Bayes," she said harshly. "We have to work with each other, and I'd quite like learn a little about you. You seem to know all about me, after all."

This time he stared at her for a long time. She could almost see clockwork behind his eyes; the bright copper cogs going round and round . . . She said as calmly as she could, "Eyes on the road."

He did as he was instructed. They were on the roundabout at the end of the road when he said, "I live with a partner."

"What's her name."

"Adrian."

It took her a moment to process this. "Ah . . ." she murmured. "Not Adrienne?"

"No."

Oh, well . . . that's that, then.

They drove on in silence into the heart of the city.

*

The house was a semi-detached near one of the university campus sites. A police constable stood at the garden gate – McFadden? McCormack? McCormick? She couldn't remember but Bayes did. He nodded and said, "McFarlane, isn't it?" The callow youth nodded, pleased to be recognised, she thought. Did Bayes have a perfect recall? She fervently hoped not. She considered him dangerous enough without such an advantage.

There were two further uniforms at the front door but Bayes didn't appear to know their names; presumably, he hadn't yet been introduced to them. They stood aside for them. For a moment, she thought Bayes was going to glad-hand them like some cheesy politician but, thank God, he didn't.

Beverley entered first and was met initially by the odour of rotting meat and then by a man in a disposable pale yellow bodysuit. At least she was sure what *his* name was. "Phelps. Tell me."

"The body's in the kitchen. Such as it is."

Beverley looked around. The house was cold and devoid of furniture. It had the smell of a house that no one had been in for many months; cold and damp, despite the bodies in their suits that wandered purposefully around.

"What does that mean?" asked Bayes.

He grimaced. "You'll see."

Bayes started in, but Beverley held up a hand. "We need suits, gloves and overshoes, first."

When they were properly attired, she commanded Phelps. "Show us."

Phelps led the way.

It wasn't so much a body, more a torso, without limbs or head. A markedly decayed and naked one at that, but undoubtedly male; the scrotum looked like a hairy red balloon. Blood and black fluid had oozed onto the light brown floor around it.

"Shit," was Bayes' first reaction. He held a gloved hand to his nose and turned away.

"Yes," said Beverley thoughtfully. She crouched down by the body, looking at it with pursed lips. "Been dead a while."

"It's rotten," was Bayes' second contribution, equally unnecessary in her opinion; the only import of the torso being "rotten" was that it meant that the perpetrator of this heinous act was long gone and that post-mortem examination would provide less information. Bayes, though, clearly meant that it was horrible to look at.

"*He's* rotten," she couldn't resist saying. Bayes didn't turn around. She stood up and turned to Phelps. "Whose house is this?"

Phelps consulted a notebook. "According to the neighbour, it's owned by a couple called 'Piper'. John and Maureen. They're living in Spain; seem to have emigrated there." He spoke as if he disapproved of this, as if it were an act of betrayal. "This place has been empty for four months, awaiting tenants."

"No one's been in here at all? Anyone from the agents?"

Phelps shrugged. He didn't know.

"How come we're here?" It wasn't a philosophical question.

"Someone came calling, presumably with an eye to a bit of B&E. What he saw through the kitchen window changed his mind."

"Anonymous call?"

Phelps nodded.

"Any chance of tracking him down?"

"Naw."

Beverley looked again at the body, then at Bayes' back. "How do you think he was dismembered, Sergeant?" Her tone was rather louder than it needed to be.

Bayes only then turned. The handkerchief was still at his nose as he cast her a baleful look. He crouched down as she had done. As he did so, she couldn't resist glancing at Phelps who had a vicious smile on his face as he watched Bayes. Bayes came around to her side of the torso. "They're very clean. No hacking involved, I'd say."

"Look at the ends of the bones."

He bent closer, then looked up at her. "A circular saw?"

"I'd say a large knife was used to cut around the flesh, and then a circular cut through the exposed bones." She looked across at Phelps, who nodded agreement with this conclusion. "Same with the head, if you look closely." She asked Phelps, "Any sign of the limbs or the head round about?"

Phelps shook his head. "Not yet. I've initiated a search of the garden."

"And house-to-house?"

"It's all ready to go. I was waiting for you, though."

"Get it started."

He nodded and left the room.

She took a deep breath. Bayes, who had continued a close inspection of the body and had moved around the torso to the opposite side, said suddenly, "This arm's different."

She moved to join him, crouching down as he stood up to give her access. "You're right. The flesh is more ragged here and – look! – there's a small saw cut in the bone closer to the shoulder, just here." She pointed with her finger; her manicure and bright crimson nail polish an interesting counterpoint to the nauseating corpse beneath it.

"What does it mean?" asked Bayes.

She didn't reply, had moved onto the neck. She murmured, "Ragged too, on this side." She moved to the other side, opposite Bayes. "And on this side, too," she murmured to herself.

She stood up. Bayes repeated his question. She was frowning. "I think that he was still alive when the first arm was removed. Hell, I think he might still have been alive when the throat was cut."

They moved back out of the kitchen to give back access to the forensics team. Phelps had returned. She asked, "Was the house secure?"

He took them to the back door and opened it. "Obviously we had to force entry at the front, and we don't know if

58

this was done by the bloke who did *that*," he gestured with his head at the torso, "Or the burglar."

She bent down, examining the deep furrows. "A screwdriver," she decided.

Bayes observed, "Not very subtle, whoever did it."

Beverley surveyed the view from the doorway. "What about the back garden?" It was a big space, perhaps a third of an acre, laid mostly to lawn with a few fruit trees dotted around and, in the far right corner, a small garden shed. The fruit trees were covered in heavy pink and white blossom.

"It looks fairly pristine," Phelps said. "I don't see the point in wasting resource on digging it up."

"Better safe than sorry." She found her phone, paged through the contacts, found one and sent it to Bayes' phone. "He owes me a favour. Use him."

Bayes was perplexed. "What for?"

"He works at the university. He has access to ground penetrating radar. The kind of stuff they use in archaeology."

"Oh . . ."

She turned back to Phelps. "Who's doing the postmortem?" she asked.

"I don't know yet."

"Get Eisenmenger."

Phelps frowned. "Hasn't he retired?"

"Get him. Whatever the cost, get him. I'll take the flack." She avoided Bayes' gaze.

Chapter Eleven

Eisenmenger pulled off his gloves and turned to Beverley and her sergeant. "There's only so much I can say without the head or limbs." They were above him, leaning over a thick Perspex screen.

"So what *can* you say?"

"The house was unheated, and it hasn't been unseasonably warm or cold, so I'd say the torso had been there for at least two months, judging by the degree of decay."

Bayes had been unaccountably absent for much of the autopsy, and was now refusing to look directly at the dismembered corpse that Neil White was busy sewing up.

"Age?"

"Tricky . . . Judging by the abdominal musculature, older than thirty, but younger than fifty, I'd say."

"Can't you be more specific?"

Beverley's question was testy, he thought. He didn't reply.

"The height's tricky, too. Assuming he didn't have achondroplasia, I'd say just above average height – perhaps one metre eighty."

Bayes asked, "Achondro . . . what?"

"Achondroplasia. Dwarfism, to be less than politically correct."

Bayes was scathing. "Of course he's not a dwarf . . ."

Eisenmenger pointed out gently, "Those with achondroplasia may have normal-sized torsos. It's only their limbs that fail to grow to a normal length."

"Do they?"

Eisenmenger continued without answering, "I think you're right in saying that the left arm was removed when he was still alive."

Bayes took a theatrically deep breath. Eisenmenger saw that Beverley was ignoring him and deduced that she was either punishing him or blooding him, or both. Whatever, it was nothing to do with him, he decided. Bayes was big enough and good-looking enough to look after himself. Beverley asked, "Any other signs of torture?"

"You're assuming that it was done as torture." Eisenmenger smiled.

"Can you think of another reason why anyone would cut off an arm while the victim was not only alive but presumably conscious?"

"*Presumably*, Detective Chief Inspector. *Presumably*. I have no evidence either way . . ." Eisenmenger had a twinkle in his eye as he said this. "I've taken samples for toxicology, but don't hold your breath, given the degree of decay."

"And was he still alive when the throat was cut?"

"Probably . . ." He looked back at the body. "Very probably . . ."

"So he went through hell before he died. Would that be a reasonable assumption, Doctor Eisenmenger?"

Again, he avoided the question. "There are a few other things . . ."

Bayes, he could see, came back from somewhere to produce a notebook at last and ask, "Such as?"

"The buttocks are inflamed."

Under other circumstances, this might have been the cue for amusement . . .

"What's the significance of that?" asked Beverley.

"Maybe nothing."

"But maybe . . . what?"

"It raises the possibility that the deceased sat in his own urine for a long time."

There was a moment's silence, into which Eisenmenger said, "And talking of the buttocks . . ."

"Yes?"

"There's a puncture mark in the right buttock. Odd place for a self-inflicted wound such as a drug addict might have."

"Meaning?"

"Perhaps that was how he was subdued enough to allow him to be restrained."

Bayes asked, "How do you know he was restrained?"

"Well, obviously, I can only make a deduction about that . . ."

Beverley interjected, "How else do you think his arm was cut off while he was still alive?" she demanded contemptuously of her sergeant. "Of course he was restrained."

Eisenmenger's look towards Bayes was full of sympathy, but ignored. He said, "The flesh of his torso bears several puncture wounds and several deep but very thin cuts."

He indicated these; one went across the right nipple, which made Bayes wince.

Beverley asked remorselessly, "What would make those kinds of wounds?"

Eisenmenger had already spent a long time thinking about this. "The puncture wounds are the kind of lesion I'd expect from an ice pick or sharpened screwdriver."

"And the cuts?"

"A razor blade or cut-throat. That kind of thing." He looked up, first at Bayes, then at Beverley, then continued, "There are also two round burns, on either side of the back of neck, just below the line of severance. They were done shortly before death and measure seven millimetres in diameter."

"Cigarette burns?"

"I'd say so. All of which would be in keeping with your torture hypothesis."

Bayes scribbled in his notebook. He waved his pencil at the torso as he asked, "Do those burns mean he was restrained in a chair with a relatively low back?"

Beverley looked at Eisenmenger who, in turn, stared at Bayes for a second. "Yes, it would suggest that."

"Why?" asked Beverley.

"Because if he was prone, the torturer would have had to turn the victim's body to reach such a site. In a chair, the back of the neck is more exposed, especially if the back of the chair only comes up to the shoulders."

"But you can't say that with any certainty."

Eisenmenger smiled. "Much of what I say has no certainty, Beverley. You know that."

"Great," said Bayes.

He was apparently disappointed; Eisenmenger wondered what he expected from forensic pathology; clearly more than reality could give. Bayes had watched too many episodes of cheesy television series, perhaps. He said, "There are numerous sores on the front and back of the torso that are interesting."

He moved over to the body; White had finished and the torso had been hosed down, showing just how decayed it was. The skin was darkened all over, but Eisenmenger pointed out several roughly circular lesions that could just be seen scattered over the skin.

"What are they?"

Eisenmenger replied, "I said they were interesting, Beverley. I didn't say I knew what they were."

For a moment, she thought he was joking, but he wasn't. "You've no idea."

"I'm not a dermatopathologist. They could be anything,

as far as I'm concerned. I'll biopsy them, but don't hold your breath, given the degree of decay."

She didn't quite say, "Shit . . ." but the look on her face was eloquent.

"You've taken samples for DNA, of course?" she asked tiredly.

He smiled at her uncertainly. "Of course and, who knows, you might get lucky and find a match."

"Well, we're not going to identify him from what we've got here," she pointed out.

Chapter Twelve

"He was tortured, then." Bayes sounded dazed. She looked at him, trying to gauge if he was safe to drive, deciding that he was.

"Apparently."

He shivered. He actually shivered. *What did you do in Tewkesbury, Bayes, that you should be so shocked? Where have you been? Man up . . .*

She looked away, out of the side window, at the grass verge rushing past. "There are only two reasons why people are tortured."

He kept his eyes on the road as he replied, "One's for information. What's the other?"

"Pleasure."

She was fairly sure that he shivered again. "Pleasure?"

She sighed. "I'm afraid so. The spirit of the Marquis de Sade is alive and well and all around us."

"*Sexual* pleasure?"

"Possibly, yes." She couldn't believe how naïve he seemed. "Who knows? Perhaps the victim was getting a buzz from being tortured." She was being cruel, she knew, but he didn't have long to get up to speed, to harden himself, or at least construct a carapace. "That's a point . . ."

"What is?"

"We need to check the websites for people advertising."

"Advertising for what?" He sounded almost fearful.

"Anyone who's interested in a sadomasochistic relationship. It's usually the sadist, but it's not unknown that the masochist advertises . . ."

He looks nauseous. I should stop, even if it is oddly fun . . .

Chapter Thirteen

Eisenmenger had debated long and hard before deciding to attend Claire Woodforde's house but, in the event, he was pleasantly surprised; he discovered that not only was she married (to a publisher) but there were five other guests. Of the six, they were split evenly between medics and non-medics, which suited him, and the food was good, too. The only thing that spoiled the evening for him was his uncertainty as to why he was there. Was he a last-minute replacement? If so, presumably for a man, since the only other singleton at the table was a woman called Rosetta. He guessed that she was a divorcee, possibly with children; they were placed together at the dinner table but she, an author of historical romances, quickly lost interest in him. She turned to the man on her left; on his right was Claire Woodforde. Inevitably, and no matter how hard he wished it otherwise, Edward Marsham's death came up.

"He was murdered," she pronounced as they were halfway through the lamb Provençale.

Eisenmenger didn't need to ask to whom she was referring. "It can't be proved," he responded simply. "Which means that it's an irrelevant assertion."

Was she mad? He couldn't decide. He was at that moment thinking that he had been unwise to accept her invitation. What had he expected would come of it?

"But taken together with the others . . ."

Her husband was deep in conversation with a woman who was, Eisenmenger dimly recalled, also an anaesthetist. Did she believe in Claire Woodforde's assertions?

"Tell me about the others . . ."

"I don't know about all of them, of course . . ."

"Of course not. But those you do know about?"

She was attacking a lamb chop and there was a delay before she replied. "I know of an old man on the respiratory ward who was getting better and expected to go home, but who died quite unexpectedly. And there was a young chap on the orthopaedic ward who was in following a motorcycle accident; he had a sudden cardiac arrest, from which he couldn't be resuscitated, which was a bit of a shock. And I've got my doubts about three other deaths."

It wasn't enough. She knew that, he could see in her eyes. He hated himself for asking, "Is that all?"

"The CQC identified an excess of eleven deaths. After I got a . . . reputation in the trust, I found it difficult to investigate any further. The IT Department came down on me heavily. They had a point; I was accessing the confidential medical information of patients and I had no right to it. I was left with my suspicions, but could do nothing about them."

"Until Marsham died."

Her smile was fleeting, as she returned her attention to the lamb chop.

After the meal, as coffee spoons stirred in coffee cups and brandy swirled in glasses, John Eisenmenger sat and took in the ambience of the house. It was expensively and tastefully furnished, and it had many photographs of Claire, a few of her husband, Matthew, and none of children. A deliberate decision or an accident of nature? He would never know, he thought; still, it was none of his business. He went to the cloakroom and, on his return, was accosted in the hallway by the man who had been sitting on the other side of Rosetta.

"John, we haven't really talked."

They had been introduced at the start of the evening. "No," agreed Eisenmenger. "It's Peter, isn't it?"

"Peter Sulston."

"You're an emergency medicine consultant, right?"

"And you're the pathologist who did a second autopsy on Mr Marsham. The one that suggested he was murdered."

Eisenmenger closed his eyes. "Not quite . . ."

But Sulston wasn't listening. "I was on duty when he first came in. I was the one who first diagnosed him as brain dead."

"I didn't say for certain that . . ."

"I was surprised by your conclusion. We'd all expected him to live a lot longer than he did, of course, but such matters are rarely predictable with any certainty."

"But . . ."

Sulston dropped his voice. "Claire's a fantastically good anaesthetist and I'd trust her with my children when it comes to intensive care, but she's on her own with this one. She's the only one to think that something funny is going on at the hospital; the only one. She's very vocal about it, and taken it a long way, but . . ."

"But what?"

He dropped his head. "She's basically behaving in an extremely irrational manner. There have been discussions, you know."

"Discussions?" Eisenmenger suspected he knew something about those "discussions". "With the CEO and COO, perchance?"

Sulston looked at him, then nodded tersely. "And the chair of the trust. Everyone agreed that she was completely wrong and that whatever the cause for the statistical anomaly . . ."

"'Statistical anomaly'? Is that what it is?"

"Conceivably, yes."

Despite himself, Eisenmenger found himself scoffing. "Of course, they're going to follow that line. They can't afford to say otherwise, can they?" He wondered why he was saying this. He didn't actually believe what Claire was saying, did he?

"There's still a total lack of proof, John."

"That people had died who shouldn't have done, or that someone's been polishing them off?"

"Both . . . Neither . . ." It struck Eisenmenger that Sulston was flustered.

Eisenmenger asked, "Can I get this straight? You're now saying that there may not be an excess of deaths?"

"That's a possibility."

"And it's the official line?"

"The trust is examining that possibility, yes."

"But it's also possible that there really *is* an excess of deaths." Sulston pursed his lips and looked unhappy, but remained silent. "In which case, it's just possible that Claire Woodforde has a point, isn't it?"

"She's wrong . . ."

"This is the kind of situation in which I get interested." He smiled, apparently at the other, but actually at his own presumption. What was it about this man that induced such hubris? Why did he want so badly to prove him wrong?

"Hence your autopsy and its results . . ."

"My autopsy indicated that it was a *possibility* that Marsham died in suspicious circumstances. It was far from the level of proof required in a criminal court, and it says nothing about any other deaths in the hospital, but I thought it intriguing enough to . . ." he stopped. Intriguing enough to what? He wasn't entirely sure; he could only surmise that it was just his nature that kept him from walking away from all of this. Sulston was looking at him.

He said, ". . . to wonder if Claire was onto something, I suppose."

Sulston made an odd noise in the back of his throat and walked away, his whole demeanour radiating disgust.

Chapter Fourteen

Lambert invaded Beverley's office the next morning and no one was very happy, least of all Lambert. "No identification at all?"

"It was a headless, limbless torso that had been in that kitchen for several weeks, sir . . ."

"What about the DNA?"

"Those results will be back in a few days, sir. As we all know, they'll be useless unless we have a match . . ."

Lambert showed characteristic disbelief, Beverley saw. He said, "And you can't identify the poor sod any other way?"

Bayes came to the rescue. "Not without a face or fingerprints."

"What about the house? Any news there?"

"The guy with the radar said that the garden had been undisturbed for a long time; probably over a year. I don't see the point in paying for the overtime in digging it up."

Lambert nodded. "What about the house-to-house?"

"What about it?" she replied. They stared at each other before Lambert abruptly stood and headed for the door. He spoke without looking back, "I want to know as soon as anything breaks."

The door slammed as he left.

Bayes looked at Beverley. "Is it me, or was that unreasonable?"

She laughed. "It was Superintendent Lambert, Bayes. Get used to it."

He returned to his task, she to hers. The websites she was trawling through made her feel slightly sick. There seemed to be hundreds of people out there who were willing to behave in ways that were at best nauseating, at worst disgusting, and plenty of them were willing to hand out – or receive – exceedingly painful punishment and torture. Feeling dirty, she sighed and sat back.

"Any luck?"

"Yes. Too much."

"You should try looking at the S&M sites," she said despondently. "Go on."

"Well, given the parameters we're searching with, I've had eighteen hits so far."

"Only eighteen?"

He looked up at her, unsure if she were being serious. "You expected more?"

"To be truthful, yes."

"Well, I haven't finished yet."

"No? You'd best keep at it, then." She smiled. "I can't see that I'm going to be able to find any gold amongst this shit . . ."

He cast a baleful look in her direction before returning to the list of missing persons.

*

Eisenmenger thought long and hard before attempting to contact Claire Woodforde with anything more than a "thank you" for the dinner. It took a while actually to get to talk to her, since he had to go through her secretary, who was in the habit of screening her calls with the aid of an answerphone. Consequently, it was several hours before he actually got to talk directly to her.

"I wanted to thank you for last night."

"Why, that's very kind of you, John."

"And . . ."

"Yes?"

"And to suggest that you might care to give me all the details you have of the patients you think might have died 'prematurely'."

There was silence for a moment. "You're sure?"

"To be honest, no . . ."

She laughed. "Stupid question. Nobody's sure. I'd welcome your opinion, though, John."

"You do realise what you're doing, don't you, Claire? I mean, even though all these people *are* dead, you'll still be in breach of the Data Protection Act."

"I appreciate that."

"And if I don't report it, so shall I."

There was a pause. "So what are you saying?"

It was his turn to hesitate. It wasn't the first time that he had broken the law in pursuit of a criminal, but never on grounds that were so flimsy. "I think I'm saying, be very careful, Claire."

Her relief was huge. "Thank you, John."

After she had promised to send him via email all she knew, and the connection was cut, he spent a long time pondering what he had done and why he had done it. Boredom, of course. It was the only answer. He was bored, and this might be something, even if it was probably nothing. That he was involved in breaking the law perhaps only added to the thrill.

The information arrived in his inbox five minutes later. He saw that it came from her private email, and not from a hospital email address.

Goodness, you're keen.

But he had known that she was a driven woman.

Driven or deluded?

There was an accompanying message.

"*Dear John,*

Thanks for agreeing to take a look at this. I know what people say about me and it is so nice not to be treated as a lunatic for once.

Kindest regards,

Claire."

*

Bayes looked up. "Twenty-six possible in total."

She reflected that it could have been worse. She asked, "Any with a criminal conviction?"

"Give me a chance, sir."

"Get onto it right away."

"May I ask why?"

"Because he was tortured. If it wasn't for pleasure, it was for information, and that information is likely to be about something illegal."

Bayes nodded slowly.

"We need to make an identification. We can't do anything without that."

He nodded. "I understand."

Beverley stood up. "While you do that, I'll get some sandwiches."

Bayes looked up in surprise. "You?"

"Yes, me. Something to say, Sergeant?"

He grinned. "I'll have ham salad on malted bread."

*

Eisenmenger looked through the information that Claire Woodforde had sent through, beginning to regret his decision to help her. She had supplied him with a spreadsheet on which were six names, each with details of the wards on which they had been placed, their diagnoses, the dates of their admission and the dates of their deaths.

What was he supposed to do with this? Was there anything he could bring to the party?

And then, having thought about it, he decided that perhaps he could.

Chapter Fifteen

"Bingo!"

One of the advantages of working at the station was the proximity of the best sandwich shop in the city. Beverley was munching contentedly on a BLT (rye) when Bayes, eating his ham sandwich (malted) while working at the computer, exclaimed thus.

She swallowed. "What is it, Sergeant?"

"One of the missing persons was Larry Davis."

The name was vaguely familiar. "What of it?"

"He had a record."

"For what?"

"Armed robbery, mostly. A bit of GBH." She remembered him. A nasty piece of work, she recalled. Tall and addicted to the gym and muscle building, which he used not only to intimidate but also to break bones.

"How long ago?"

"His last conviction was three years ago. He went to Wakefield. A fifteen-year stretch."

"How come he's on the missing persons' list, then?"

"He broke out four months ago – or was broken out."

Of course. How could she forget? He hadn't been recaptured and there was still an alert out on him. The most missing of missing persons. She asked, "He was tortured because . . .?"

Bayes appeared to think the question stupid. "Because whoever broke him out wanted to find out where he had hidden the money from his last robbery."

It all sounded a bit tired and clichéd to Beverley, but she said nothing to discourage him. Clichés were clichés because they happened often, after all. "We'll have his DNA on record, then."

"Should have."

"So, if you're right, we'll have a match tomorrow."

"I suppose so."

"That doesn't mean you stop looking now."

He frowned and was perhaps about to argue before thinking better of it and returning to his task.

*

"I need more, Claire."

"Oh . . . Like what?"

"I need direct access to the medical records. What you've sent through just isn't enough."

He knew that what he was asking was difficult, if not impossible.

"What are you looking for?"

"I don't know." Which was the truth. He'd know it when he found it – *if* he found it – but not until then. That was the way of things with John Eisenmenger. If she didn't like it, well, she didn't like it; he had very little invested in this, other than an escape from boredom.

She thought long and hard. "Neither do I, John . . ." she said at last. "I can't just take the notes."

"Then get me to the notes."

Again she had to think about this. "How?"

"Leave them in your office, then let me in for an hour or so. You needn't be there."

For a third time, he heard nothing on the line as she thought about this.

"Okay. Tomorrow at seven. My office."

"Where is it?"

"I'll send you a map."

"From your personal email, don't forget. We don't want to leave an easy trail, Claire."

"No, no." Was it his imagination, or did she now sound unsure? Was he asking too much of her?

Tough shit. You started this.

*

"Three more with criminal convictions." Bayes sounded disappointed, but not greatly so. "All minor, though."

"Let me see."

He sent them to her computer. She perused them while

he looked at her she thought, like a young puppy. It wasn't a look she found particularly uncomfortable. She said thoughtfully, "Very minor."

"Exactly."

"Vagrancy, drunk and disorderly, breach of the peace . . ."

"Exactly." He sounded pleased with himself.

She returned to her computer screen and thought some more about what it all might mean.

Chapter Sixteen

The next evening, at seven p.m., Eisenmenger let himself into Claire Woodforde's office, feeling like a thief. It was small and disordered and smelled of damp; there were two desks but she had warned him that she shared the office with another consultant anaesthetist, so this was no surprise to him. The window looked down onto a frailty ward and, fascinating as it was to see into their dirty utility room, he kept away from it as soon as he became aware of it. Despite the piles of paper that were scattered around the office – Eisenmenger counted at least seven – the worn green folders of varying thickness that were piled in the centre of the desk to the right – which she had told him was hers – were immediately apparent. He pulled down the blinds while standing to one side, took out an A4 notebook and began to leaf through the clinical notes.

*

"It's not Davis, then."

Bayes sounded offended. Beverley knew the feeling. She said, "No."

The DNA results had come in via email only twenty minutes ago. There was no match with Larry Davis. The DNA sample suggested that their victim was Emile Durkheim, one of the others on Bayes' list.

"Durkheim was arrested multiple times," mused Beverley. "Drunk and disorderly, and vagrancy mostly."

"At least Lambert will be happy that we've got an identification of the torso."

"Suddenly this case is looking a lot harder, though," she said thoughtfully.

"It is? Why?"

"Because I don't believe that Emile Durkheim was tortured for anything he knew – what would a tramp know? – which means he was tortured for pleasure."

"So?"

"That means it's going to be a lot harder to find who did it." She thought of the S&M sites, but then brightened up. Emile Durkheim would have been very unlikely to have access to the worldwide web. While she thought about this, she returned to the computer. Durkheim, forty-nine years old, originally from France. He had come to the UK in the early years of the millennium, a mid-level banker. He had lost his job in 2009, hit the bottle, and gradually lost everything. He had had a diagnosis of epilepsy made in 2014 in London, been picked up thereafter in various parts of the country. Last definitely identified at the Royal Infirmary six months ago when he had been admitted with hypothermia.

Bayes said suddenly, "Perhaps he saw something. Something that meant he had to die."

"Then he wouldn't have been tortured."

He tried again. "He could have been tortured by another group trying to find out what he knew."

She bit down on a withering response. Where did he get his ideas from, she wondered? *The Valiant*? It wouldn't be long before he started prattling on about the "Black Hand Gang", and Sexton Blake and the Yellow Peril . . .

She said mildly, "I don't think so, Sergeant. I'm afraid he was tortured because somebody wanted him to experience as much pain as they could inflict on him."

"That's horrible."

"Did you contact the agents?"

"They last went to the house on the eleventh of the month before last. Ten weeks ago."

"I assume that there was nothing untoward?"

"No body in the kitchen, if that's what you mean."

She looked at him sharply, unable for the moment to decide if he were being sarcastic. She said levelly, "And the house was secure?"

"Apparently."

"Ten weeks ago . . . Combined with what John Eisenmenger said, that would suggest that the torso was put in the house not long after the house was last visited."

Bayes asked, "Which could be chance or . . ."

"Or the house was being watched . . ." They looked at each other. "Anything at all from the house-to-house?"

"Nobody saw anything."

She laughed bitterly. "They so rarely do."

*

Eisenmenger left Claire Woodforde's office at eight-thirty. He walked quickly along the main corridor of the infirmary, marvelling at how it was different from and yet entirely similar to a hundred other hospital corridors that, over the decades, he'd spent many hours in. This one was relatively newly built with green painted walls, signs to various hospital departments on the walls, interspersed with historical photographs. The floor was scuffed, as all hospital floors were. At this time of evening, it was nearly empty and this brought back memories of nights on call when he had been a junior doctor; life and medicine had been very different then; simpler, perhaps. These thoughts occupied him completely, for he could remember the emotions he had held within him then with stunning force; anxiety amounting almost to fear, pride and dislocation.

"Watch out, mate."

So deep had been his reverie, he had not seen the intersection coming up, and he had almost collided with a porter pushing an empty wheelchair along the crossing corridor.

"Sorry . . ." Had it been his fault? He couldn't say. The porter seemed to think so, but then generally speaking other people in this situation usually did.

"You were in a dream." This was thrown over the shoulder of the porter, who obviously had some important task to complete as he hurried towards somewhere. Eisenmenger was thus accused, as if it were a crime. He turned left, in the opposite direction to the porter, as much to get away from him as to follow his original intention which was to get out. He found himself in the Emergency Department and, before he could escape from there, he was spotted.

"John! What are you doing here?"

It was Peter Sulston, dressed now in dark green scrubs with spots of blood on the front of his chest. He was sitting at a desk in the middle of the department, with cubicles all around, some closed off by curtains, some open and empty. There were perhaps six others in the room, some also sitting but some standing. They all looked at Eisenmenger. "Wrong turn," he replied, flustered. "Sorry."

"You're trying to get out?" Sulston stood. He was a tall man – giving Eisenmenger perhaps five centimetres – and from the reaction of the others, he was the leader in the room. "Let me direct you."

"I don't want to take you away from . . ."

"It's quiet." Sulston would not be put off. "It won't be in three hours or so, but we take our rest when we can. This way."

He didn't actually touch Eisenmenger, but the pathologist felt compelled to follow Sulston. Once they were back in the corridor, Sulston turned to him. "What are you doing here so late, John?"

Eisenmenger didn't want to say. He didn't have to, though, for Sulston said, "Working on Claire's loony hypothesis?" He was smiling.

"Something like that."

Sulston looked up and down the corridor. "Be careful, John. She's a very earnest lady whose heart is in the right place, but you wouldn't be the first to be hurt because she drew you into her fantasies."

They looked at one another. Eisenmenger saw friendly concern on Sulston's face, but he wondered if there were something else beneath; something that was less friendly, if not to Eisenmenger, then to Claire Woodforde. Was he trying to cover something up? Eisenmenger's notebook, held now under his arm, contained oddities that he had noted and that, if viewed with a particular frame of mind, could chime with Claire Woodforde's outlandish hypothesis.

"Thanks for the advice, Peter."

Peter held his gaze for a moment longer before there came a laugh from him that broke the tension. "There's nothing so unwanted as unwanted advice," he said. "Here. This is the way out."

Chapter Seventeen

"May I come in, John?"

He stood to one side. "Of course. Sorry I was out earlier."

She entered his house. He was immediately aware that it was the first time that Beverley had been inside this house; he was also immediately reminded that she was a police officer to her bones, for she looked around her with rapt concentration. "What do you think?" The question was out there before he realised it.

She turned and smiled, nodded, looked around, then looked back at him. "This bit's nice."

They both laughed as he thought the adjective a little insipid, and he heard an unspoken word at the end of her sentence.

Inevitably, he asked, "But?"

Dropping her voice slightly although still smiling, she

said, "But nothing, John. Don't be paranoid." He dropped his head. She walked to the front window. "Nice neighbours?" she asked, peering out.

"We get on well. They're very helpful."

"Good. That's important."

She turned back to him and took off her leather jacket. She handed it to him. He took it and hung it by the front door. When he turned around, she was already seated in the sofa, her legs crossed. "Coffee?" he asked. He couldn't help but look at her covetously.

"White wine."

Of course.

He returned with a bottle in a chiller and two glasses that he put down on the coffee table. Once he would have sat beside her, now he sat in an armchair. "What can I do for you?" He set out the glasses and opened the wine as he spoke.

"Can't it be a social call? For old time's sake?"

"Is it?"

She pursed her lips like he wanted to kiss him. "Well . . . Maybe . . ."

He shook his head. "That's a 'no', then. So why are you here, Beverley?"

He'd never called her "Bev", always "Beverley", which she liked.

"We've made progress with our torso."

Pouring out the wine, he asked, "You've identified it?"

She told him, then asked, "Those odd things on the skin. Could they be bites from bed bugs?"

"Some sort of arthropod bite, yes."

"What's an arthropod?"

"Insects are arthropods." She looked at him over the rim of her glass. "What?" he asked.

"You've always been like that."

"Like what?"

She leaned forward and put down the glass. As he watched her, he tried to suppress the feelings of desire. She leaned back and looked at him. "I could never work out whether you used long, scientific words because you were anally retentive or just pompous."

He thought about this, trying not to be offended, and trying to work out if she were goading him and, if so, why. "And since we split, have you come to a conclusion?"

She laughed it off. "It makes sense, given that he was a down-and-out."

"And therefore all but invisible."

"Exactly. Who cares if a vagrant goes missing?"

"So why was he tortured? Just because he could be?"

"It's the most likely explanation."

He leaned forward, picked up his glass, took a mouthful of wine. "Have you any idea why he was dismembered and left in that particular house?"

"This is good wine," she said. "Pouilly-Fumé?"

"You're right. I'm impressed."

She sighed. "Are you patronising me, John?"

"It can't be to stop him being identified."

"Not having a head or fingerprints did make it rather difficult."

"But not impossible. In this age of DNA analysis, you got an identity and full history within a few days. And that was from a seriously decayed body."

"You have another theory about why he'd had his limbs and head sawn off?"

He had retrieved his glass and now took another large sip. "I was thinking it might be because they'd be relatively easy to dispose of."

"Go on."

"You don't need a large incinerator to burn them in, especially if you saw the limbs in half . . ." He stopped suddenly.

"Why not cut up the torso, then?"

It took him a while to respond, then he shrugged. "Messy. All those abdominal organs, all that shit in the gut . . ."

"Thanks for that image."

He smiled. He knew that she wasn't squeamish. "It could be an acid bath, of course."

"Pardon?"

"It wasn't necessarily incineration. The limbs and head could have been dissolved in acid."

She stared at him, but he was somewhere else. He sighed and then said, "I also wonder if speed was a factor."

"Explain that."

"Rapid disposal of the body."

"Maybe."

"You don't like the hypothesis."

She drained her glass. "Not much."

Having refilled their glasses, he said, "Tell me your ideas, then."

"It must have been done in a remote house . . ."

"Because of the screams?" She nodded. "Unless it was done in a soundproof room. Then it could have been done anywhere. Even in the middle of a town or city."

She glanced sharply at him, but said only, "You know what really worries me, John?"

"Tell me."

"The torso was two months old."

He looked at her, nodding slowly. "There are others?"

"If this guy was tortured for pleasure, then there must be. He wouldn't have stopped at one. We just haven't found them yet."

She stayed the night and he lay awake in the bed next to her, wondering many things. By the time morning came, he had made his mind up about a good deal of them. She rose early and showered; then returned to the bedroom to dress while he went into the en suite shower room. They didn't speak of the night just passed at all, as if ashamed of it. He searched his feelings; he, at least, didn't feel ashamed, he decided. He hoped she felt likewise.

They were both in the kitchen when he looked her in the eye for the first time that morning. "I need a favour."

She put down her coffee mug, raising eyebrows that were characteristically pencil thin. Her expression was amused. "Yes, John?"

He left the kitchen, returning a moment later with his

notes from the hospital. "Look through these. Tell me what you think."

She took the notebook. "What's this about?"

"You remember Edward Marsham, of course . . ."

"I do."

"And how we're uncertain if he died by his own hand, or if someone had a hand in it . . ."

"I said I remembered, John. What of it?"

He explained about Claire Woodforde and her theory that someone was killing patients at the infirmary. He was relieved that she didn't laugh, at least. He said, "I'd value your opinion."

She put the notebook down on the table in front of her. "Oh, come on, John."

"No hurry, Beverley," he interrupted quickly.

She closed her mouth for a second, then tried a smile, then dropped it when she saw the pleading look on his face. "There's a sicko out there who's tortured and killed someone. That's real. This isn't."

"It might be," he said but he was aware how pathetic it sounded.

"Tell me when it definitely is, then." She pushed it back.

It stayed between them, untouched.

As she left, he said, "Beverley . . ."

She turned. That smile was playing around her lips again and he had the feeling that she knew exactly what he was going to say. "Yes, John?"

He said it anyway. "About last night . . ."

"What about it?"

But words failed him. He looked at her for what seemed like a long time, then shrugged, smiled weakly and said, "Nothing."

She nodded thoughtfully. "Exactly," she said quietly.

Chapter Eighteen

"Where are we, Chief Inspector?" Lambert – never one to radiate bonhomie – looked as if he had swallowed an angry hornet, and it had made its way to his colon, sting intact, as mad as hell. Beverley decided that he wasn't talking metaphysically or literally.

She said, "We have an identity for the deceased, sir."

"Yes." He looked at his computer screen. Neither Beverley nor Bayes, on opposite sides of the desk, could see it. "Emile Durkheim."

Bayes piped up from his side, "A French ex-banker."

Lambert wasn't taking prisoners, which gave Beverley a small amount of schadenfreude. "You think that's significant, Sergeant?" he demanded. He didn't sound friendly.

If Bayes had hoped to feel the light of approval shining warm upon his skin, Beverley saw that he was disabused by the tone. She didn't allow the smile to surface, though;

she knew better than that. Bayes faltered under Lambert's scrutiny. "Possibly . . ."

Lambert swung round to Beverley. "Do you?"

"I doubt it. He hasn't been in banking for over eight years."

"And his nationality?"

"What about it?"

He stared at her. She stared back. She said, "I think it's of far more significance that he was a vagrant."

Lambert thought about this. He said slowly, "He had been there for ten weeks . . ."

". . . At most, sir." If Bayes hoped to take cover in the green zone of Lambert's approval with that interruption, he was mistaken.

Lambert closed his eyes. Beverley's smile twitched into life but had sensibly died before the superintendent opened them again. He continued, "You know what this means?" He looked at Beverley.

She said, "There are more."

He nodded grimly. "There are more."

Bayes said unwisely, "That's not necessarily a bad thing."

They both turned to him, Beverley with raised eyebrows, Lambert with an expression more akin to angry disbelief. He asked, "Enlighten me, Bayes."

Spotting that he had made a tactical mistake, Bayes replied uncertainly, "There'll be more forensic evidence, for a start. And . . ."

But Lambert silenced him with a wave of his hand.

"Never voice that kind of comment outside of this station, Sergeant. Never."

"Oh, no, I would never . . ."

"Good." Lambert turned away from him towards Beverley. "What about the owners of the house?" He looked at his computer screen. "The Pipers . . ." He looked back to her. "Are they likely to be involved?"

"I don't believe so, sir. I think the house was chosen because it was empty. Nothing more."

"So what now?" he asked. They had reached the point of the meeting.

"I want your permission to go public with the deceased's identity, sir. Then we can perhaps piece together the last few days of his life."

His frown took a moment to gather but, when it did, it was a thing of dangerous beauty, she saw, like a twister forming on the horizon. "You don't need it, Chief Inspector. You know that. You're of sufficiently high rank to do that anyway."

"If we do, it's likely that we'll generate a lot of press interest. I'll need some help."

And help had resource implications, which was why she was clearing it with him first. He considered. "You can have a detective constable."

"Just one?" She tried to keep incredulity from her voice. She didn't entirely succeed.

"Take Frazier."

"Frazier?"

"Something wrong, Chief Inspector?"

Lee Frazier was a lazy, racist, homophobic slob, with an eighteen-inch neck and unpleasant bodily habits, so there was plenty wrong, but nothing she was about to mention to Lambert. He smiled at her, because he knew exactly what he was doing. He might only have been at the station for a few days, but he knew all right.

Bastard . . .

She stood. Bayes stood as well. They went to the door, Bayes leading. Lambert called out, "Wharton?"

She turned in the doorway. "Yes, Sir?"

"You've got two weeks."

"Sir?"

"You've got two weeks to clear this up."

She moved back into the room. "Otherwise . . .?"

"Otherwise, I'll take the case from you."

She thought about arguing, but walked out in silence. She was just at the door when he called to her, "And a word of advice, DCI."

She turned warily. "Sir?"

"Don't release too many details."

"Sir?"

"There's no need to mention that that we're dealing with torsos, and certainly don't mention the torture or Eisenmenger's lurid theories about dismemberment and beheading whilst the victims were still alive."

"How do I explain the lack of progress with identification?"

He thought about this. "The degree of decay."

She could see where he was coming from, although it would make her job difficult, she thought. "Very well, sir."

Bayes was waiting in the corridor at a diplomatic distance. Maybe he hadn't heard. Maybe he had. They walked back to their office in silence.

Chapter Nineteen

"She's so bloody difficult." Bayes sighed.

"You knew she would be, Tom."

Bayes laughed. "And then there's Lambert."

"Who's he?"

"Our superintendent."

"Is he difficult, too?"

Bayes looked at his partner. There were times when Adrian made him want to scream. Usually it was because, as now, he didn't seem able to empathise with what Bayes had to go through in the police force. "Yes," he said flatly.

Adrian shrugged. He handed the dish of potatoes to Tom. "More?"

Bayes took it and helped himself. Adrian asked, "It's good, isn't it?"

"Very."

"I got the recipe from the *Sunday Times*."

"It's very nice."

Adrian dropped his head, kept on eating, not trusting himself to respond to Bayes' half-hearted compliment. They finished the meal in silence. Unexpectedly, Bayes put out his hand to envelop Adrian's. When he looked up in surprise, Bayes was smiling. "Thanks. It was delicious."

"Bad day?"

"If only it was. I've got a horrible feeling, though, that it was a *normal* day."

"Regretting the transfer?" Adrian had been in two minds about his move. Only two years out from testicular cancer, Adrian had become noticeably more timid about everything, in Tom Bayes' opinion., and he sometimes found it irritating.

"It's early days."

Adrian stood up and began to clear the plates. Tom could tell that he wasn't happy, even though the expression on his face was studiedly neutral. Bayes watched him leave the dining room for the kitchen, his hands full. He felt guilty for bringing his work troubles home to Adrian; he tried so very hard not to, but sometimes circumstances overwhelmed him.

He stood up and collected the dishes that his partner had been unable to carry. In the kitchen, Adrian was stacking the dishwasher. "Sorry," he said to Adrian's back. Adrian turned and they held each other.

"What kind of a day did *you* have? How was *your* office?"

Adrian laughed. "Very, very boring. Wonderfully so. No headless, limbless torsos. Nothing rotted at all."

*

Eisenmenger had taken photocopies of the notes he had taken in Claire Woodforde's office and these he now read and reread obsessively. At the end of the day, he was, he had to admit, an obsessive. It had infuriated Helena, he knew, just as it had infuriated Maria before her. And, once upon a time, his wife, he guessed. Had it affected Beverley likewise? They probably weren't together long enough. He could only hope.

He was who he was.

Obsessive. Screwed up. Weird. Damaged.

Oh, yes, he knew that he was damaged. Damaged by what he could not stop doing. Flashbacks and obsession with things that normal people shut away. A headless, limbless torso; a man whom he believed had been tortured by having his arm cut off; who had been alive when his decapitation was started; a body remnant that had been badly rotted. It was supposed to be to him all just a day's work.

Not *just*, though. A day's work that would leave him with a variant of post-traumatic stress.

Yet he was addicted, as much as a shamefaced attender at an AA or GA meeting was; he was no better than a chain-smoker, except that his guilty pleasure was death and murder, and what they might do to a human being by way of physical changes to the body.

He sipped some coffee – no wine that night – and read through his notes for perhaps the eighth time. The deaths

– individually prosaic – held a secret, he knew, but he couldn't see what it was with clarity. Even if Peter Sulston and the senior managers of the trust mocked Claire Woodforde, he would continue to believe that there was something odd about it all, because that was who he was.

What, though, was there to see? The deaths had few things in common – all male, all emergency admissions, and all conceivably the result of an injection of potassium chloride or some such. *Any* death, though, was conceivably the result of an injection of potassium chloride, or morphine sulphate, or insulin, or any number of things. Without the benefit of a full forensic post-mortem, it was conceivably possible to kill in so many ways; but in a hospital, where the drugs were stored, and so carefully accounted for . . .?

Potassium chloride wasn't a controlled drug.

He picked up his mobile phone and, from the contacts, called Claire Woodforde. She didn't pick up for a long time and he thought it was going to go to voicemail, but after several long moments she answered. She was out of breath and he knew at once that she had been making love. He felt uncomfortable.

"Claire? It's John Eisenmenger . . ."

"Oh . . . John. Of course . . ." He heard that her tone was shot through with a mix of tiredness and irritation.

"If it's not convenient . . ."

There was some hesitation in which he could not stop his imagination filling in unwanted details. She replied eventually, and with audible uncertainty, "It's fine. What do you want?"

"I need the nursing and portering rosters for the Emergency Department."

"You've found something?" she was at once excited.

"I don't know, and I won't know until I see the rosters. Can you get them?"

"Yes . . ." She sounded unsure. "Yes, I think so. How far back?"

"The whole year."

"A year?" Her enthusiasm was suddenly gone. "Wow, I don't know . . ."

"I know it won't be easy, Claire . . ."

She sighed. "No, no. Of course. I'll see what I can do."

He broke the connection, feeling embarrassed and almost dirty, almost as if he had physically intruded into her private life.

Chapter Twenty

The call came at four o'clock in the morning, waking him
from a deep sleep.

"John, we need you."

It was Beverley's voice. If she'd said, 'I', things would
have been so different.

"Where are you?" he asked tiredly.

"In hell."

He knew at once what she meant. "How many?"

"Six."

The postcode she gave him brought him to allotments.
He would have thought that was a mistake but for the
police cars at the end of the track. They held him up while
they checked his identity and he got cold in the early
morning sunlight, then let him through with an escort. Not
that he needed one. The source of all the fuss was quite
obvious in the dawn, for there was nothing else to see

across the flat field that had been turned into multiple allotments.

He walked with the female police officer; they made no conversation. He tried to warm himself, but he didn't succeed, and then he forgot his chill anyway, when they approached the northeast corner of the field. They had walked past runner beans that were climbing up bamboo poles, potatoes showing through the tops of furrowed earth, onions waving green leaves in the slightest of breezes, and delicate carrot leaves doing likewise. Now they were at a chain-link fence, where there were two more uniformed police officers standing either side of a ragged, curved cut in it; it would be possible to get through the fence here. Beyond it was a jungle of heavily overgrown and neglected shrubs, through which Eisenmenger could just make out a sort of track. It had rained in the night and in the soft mud he could see a lot of recent boots had made their mark.

"Through there?" he asked.

His companion nodded. "Through there."

She clearly wasn't joking; she clearly wasn't the *type* to joke. He ducked down as one of the other police constables held the crude chain-link door to one side. The female police officer followed him. They still made no conversation. It was a short journey through the sodden shrubs that were only too happy to shed rain water onto his Parka, and then they were into a garden.

At first sight, it was packed with police. Eisenmenger

counted over ten, both in and out of uniform. Beverley was there, as was Bayes, standing beside a small, decrepit shed, each dressed in pale blue forensic suits, the hoods down, their feet encased in overshoes. The lawn looked as if a tank had done exuberant manoeuvres on it. There was a derelict house beyond and a stink to the air.

Beverley approached him. "They're in the shed." He opened his mouth but she interrupted him. "Before you ask, there's no way in through the house. The floorboards are rotten; Phelps nearly broke his leg when he tried."

He indicated the lawn and the path along which he had just come. "Don't fancy your chances of getting much forensic evidence from all this."

Her expression and gaze held him. "We got what we could as soon as we realised what we had here." He could hear annoyance in her tone, as if he had been questioning her professionalism; it spoke to him of insecurity. It was a familiar feeling.

He was handed a disposable boiler suit and overshoes, which he put on with the aid of Bayes. He approached the shed, aware that everyone was looking at him. The stink increased and, when he opened the shed door, became palpable. It was nearly falling down, might well have done so had it not been stacked floor to corrugated iron ceiling with limbless, headless torsos in varying degrees of decay.

Lambert arrived an hour later, clearly put out that he had to approach the scene of the crime by such a circuitous route. A marquee had been erected alongside the shed and the torsos had been laid out on a dark green tarpaulin. The house to which the garden belonged was in the middle of a terrace, and all were derelict, so that there was a reasonable degree of privacy, although the police presence had inevitably drawn a crowd, at either end of the short street, that was growing as the day grew older and the news spread.

"What have we got?" Eisenmenger heard the familiar voice – its accustomed peremptory anger – as he worked inside the marquee.

"Six torsos. They were neatly stacked in that shed by someone."

"Six?" Lambert sounded unbelieving, as if Beverley might be pulling his leg, an inappropriate joke in such a place.

"Six," she confirmed.

"Christ." Although under Lambert's breath, this was still clearly audible. "Who owns the house?"

"City Holdings." This was Bayes' voice. "They're a subdivision of City and Suburbia."

"And who are they when they're at home?"

"Property developers. This whole terrace was due for demolition."

"To build what?"

"A petrol filling station, I think."

Eisenmenger emerged from the marquee. Perhaps it was the waft of putrefaction he brought with him that caused Lambert's face to wrinkle in disgust. "Doctor Eisenmenger." His voice held its usual sour tone.

"Superintendent Lambert." Eisenmenger didn't have to be obsequious and wasn't about to be. He removed his disposable gloves. "It's been a while."

"What can you tell us?"

"Six torsos, exactly as the first in that they've been beheaded and dismembered. All male. They're in different states of decay, with the oldest at the bottom . . ."

Bayes said excitedly, "So they were killed in order?"

"I'd say so, yes."

"At regular intervals?"

Eisenmenger looked back at the marquee. "Possibly."

Lambert was eager. "Can you say how long the intervals were?"

He turned back to Lambert. "No. And it may not be at regular intervals. I said it was only a possibility."

Lambert gave him a dirty look which Eisenmenger ignored. He said, "There was a lot of predation . . ."

"Rats," explained Beverley. "There have been complaints for weeks to the council about the rat problem around here. Now we know why."

"How did it come to light?" asked Eisenmenger.

Bayes explained. "City Holdings were doing some preliminary survey work in the garden next door. It was the smell, of course."

"Any evidence of torture?" It was Lambert's question.

"Too early to say, given the state of decay of most of the torsos."

Lambert looked disgusted, as if this were the minimum

he should have been able to tell them. Eisenmenger began to remove his suit. Whilst he was doing so, he said, "This isn't the end of it, by the way."

"What does that mean?" demanded Lambert.

Eisenmenger stood up, the suit around his ankles. "Because it was a small shed and it was full, and the newest body in there was more decayed than Emile Durkheim . . . . That's why the killer had to find somewhere else to get rid of him."

It took him a while to get out of the over-suit, but he eventually managed it, albeit slightly out of breath. Beverley said, "So you think that somewhere there are more bodies?"

"Unless the killer stopped ten weeks ago." He smiled grimly. "Which I doubt . . ."

Chapter Twenty-One

"You've taken DNA samples?"

"From all of them, yes."

The stench in the dissection room was, literally, eye-watering; Bayes was outside. Lambert hadn't even made his way to the mortuary. Only Beverley now looked down from the viewing gallery, surveying the grisly scene as torsos lay everywhere, as though a portal to Hades had opened up and deposited them on all available surfaces.

"Any conclusions you'd care to share at this point?" she asked, as Bayes returned, his demeanour timid and tentative. He did nothing until she glared at him, whereupon he produced a notebook that he concentrated on with unnatural ferocity.

Eisenmenger sighed. "No definitive cause of death on any, I'm afraid."

"Any evidence that any of them were vagrants, like Durkheim?"

He turned and walked to one of the torsos. "You see these linear marks here?" He was pointing at the stomach.

She didn't but said anyway, "What about them?"

"They could be scabies tracks. It certainly looks as if they were itchy."

Bayes asked, his head still down, "Meaning?"

"Anyone can get scabies – it's unbelievably contagious – but it tends to be a . . . shall we, say, *lower class* thing."

"I had it once," murmured Beverley. "I got it because I went under cover and had to sleep rough for a couple of weeks." *That* made Bayes look up.

"And two of them had sores similar to the first torso," continued Eisenmenger. "As well as being undernourished."

"So at least three of them were likely to have been down and out."

Eisenmenger said, "What a quaint term."

"Quaint or not, it would be in keeping with the killer's MO."

"Two of them would have been clinically obese, if not morbidly obese, I'd say." Eisenmenger sounded apologetic. "Hardly your usual tramp."

She had to admit that he was probably right; she didn't have to enjoy the experience, though. "Maybe not."

"All six of them have inflamed buttocks."

"They sat in their own urine?"

"For a long time."

"What does 'for a long time' mean?" enquired Bayes.

"I'd guess days."

Beverley absorbed this with a shake of her head. "Anything else?"

"Yes. Three of them had something wrong with them."

"What does that mean?"

"One had a healing gastric ulcer, another had a small lung cancer in his left lung, another had quite severe chronic obstructive pulmonary disease."

"Is that a surprise?"

He shrugged. "Maybe not."

"Were they tortured?"

Eisenmenger nodded. "By a variety of means, I'd say."

"Go on."

He turned and indicated one on the far side of the room. It was the most decayed and rat-bitten. "That was on the bottom of the pile so we can assume that he was the first. There's no indication that he had any of his limbs removed while he was still alive . . ."

"Thank heavens for small mercies . . ."

"But he was cut quite deeply in several areas with a very thin blade."

"The razor blade again?"

"Looks like it." He gestured again. "That one beyond, was on top of the pile. He was the least putrefied."

"The last in."

"Exactly. On his body is a combination of cigarette

burns, cuts and puncture wounds of some type. Very similar to those seen on Emile Durkheim."

She thought for a moment while he looked at her, as if waiting. When she next spoke, it was in a low voice. "Tell me what this means, John."

He was smiling, but it wasn't a cheerful thing that he had on his face. "The torture goes on for days, and it's getting worse. Our man's getting a taste for it."

Chapter Twenty-Two

Beverley stood in front of a whiteboard, but she was looking at Bayes and Frazier as they sat around her. Frazier had been moved into their already cramped office, his desk opposite Bayes to the left of Beverley. The whiteboard formed the fourth wall of a square. It was blank; she held a red "wipe-clean" marker pen. She commanded, "Talk to me, you two." But she could see that they didn't know what to say. She explained, "We won't know what we know until it's written down up here. We share theories, ideas, arguments. Maybe you two have some hypothesis that I don't; maybe you've seen something I've missed."

Frazier looked lost.

Bayes said slowly, "We have seven bodies . . ."

"Headless, limbless torsos." She wrote this down.

"At present we have only one of them identified – Emile Durkheim. His history suggests that he had become a vagrant." As Bayes said this, Beverley drew a line down at the end of which she wrote Durkheim's name.

Frazier piped up. She nodded at him in encouragement as he said, "At least three of the others may have been tramps as well." She drew a parallel line and then "*3 other tramps?*"

She said thoughtfully, "Durkheim had been a banker. Perhaps the killer had something against bankers." She wrote *banker* by Durkheim's name.

"Maybe the killer lost a lot of money in the 2008 crash." Bayes was excited as this occurred to him. His face almost shone, Beverley thought. She didn't think much of it as a hypothesis, but she was too experienced to dismiss it without at least looking a little further into it. "Check up on Durkheim's old colleagues," she ordered. "Make sure that they're safe and sound."

He wrote this down. She returned to the whiteboard and looked at it. "The first six in an abandoned garden shed, and then the seventh in the kitchen of an empty house, if we go by the states of decay."

There was a large map of the city on the wall; Bayes had dutifully marked the position of the shed and the kitchen on it with pins, but it was all meaningless without a third location to triangulate things and, even then, the triangulation might well prove to be spurious.

From behind her, Frazier said, "We know why, though."

She turned. "Why what?"

"Why the killer put the seventh somewhere else and not in the shed."

"Because the shed was full."

"Exactly."

"The kitchen wasn't full."

"I'm sorry?" Frazier wasn't really sorry, but she wasn't about to argue.

"The kitchen wasn't full," she repeated.

"So?"

"There was only one torso in the kitchen. It was probably ten weeks old. I don't believe that the killer stopped after Durkheim, do you? They never do."

Frazier frowned. All two hundred and ten pounds of him. "No . . ."

"So why didn't he leave the others in the kitchen?"

Frazier had nothing to say but she could see that Bayes was considering this. He said slowly, "Maybe he *did* stop . . ."

She shook her head. "Serial killers never stop of their own accord, especially this type, the ones who are getting a kick out of it. They have to be stopped."

"That's what I mean. Perhaps he *was* stopped . . ."

She frowned. "What do you mean?" Frazier, thank goodness, contented himself with looking at Bayes without comment.

"Perhaps he died."

Well, she had to admit, she couldn't definitely exclude that possibility. Not that she believed it for one second. "We can't afford to rely on that," she said mildly. "Can we?"

Perhaps he thought he had been clever, for she had the distinct impression he was about to argue, but then thought better of it. "I guess not."

"So why hasn't he used the kitchen again? And where are the other bodies?" She wrote these questions on the whiteboard. Then, just for completeness, she wrote in small letters, "*Is the killer dead?*"

Frazier voiced an opinion. "He must have got the body in there in the dead of night."

"Presumably."

Bayes chipped in. "But the chances of being seen were still quite high. Maybe the killer decided it was too dangerous to go back."

Beverley nodded. "That sounds reasonable. Certainly, it's nowhere near as secluded as the shed was."

They all looked at the whiteboard in silence. She said, "And why remove the limbs and the head? Was it merely to make identification harder?"

"Surely the killer would know that it wouldn't make it impossible, though," Bayes said.

"Was John Eisenmenger right?" she mused.

"What's his theory?" Frazier's tone was sarcastic.

She went to the whiteboard and wrote, "*Why cut off the limbs and heads?*" Only then did she turn back to Bayes and Frazier. "That it's relatively easy to dispose of limbs and heads, not so with the torsos."

"Do you believe that?"

"No. Not really."

Bayes asked tentatively with a glance at Frazier, "It couldn't be terrorist, could it? You know, Islamic . . ."

"What makes you say that?" But it wasn't necessarily a bad question. Terrorism had always to be considered.

He bowed his head, as if ashamed of raising the subject. Frazier, the fat slob, looked on with a smile. She said, "I think that if it was, we'd know about it by now."

Bayes nodded. "You're right, of course."

They stared again at the whiteboard but no further illumination came to any of them. She put the marker pen in the narrow tray at the bottom of the board and then sat down heavily behind her desk. Bayes went over to Frazier's desk to compare notes. Then he began to investigate Durkheim's past as a banker.

Chapter Twenty-Three

"I think I've managed to get what you want. I'll send it over."

Claire Woodforde's voice was hushed as if she were trying to make the phone call in secret and Eisenmenger wondered if she were unwise enough to call him while not alone in the office. He couldn't escape the feeling which, in truth, was never far from his thoughts, that she was totally loopy.

He tried not to whisper as he replied. "Thanks, Claire."

"It wasn't easy, John."

"I'm very grateful."

"I hope I haven't drawn attention to myself . . ."

What did this woman want? "I'm sure you haven't." Although he had no evidence of this.

"I hope not."

He refused to feel guilty. He hadn't asked to get involved, so why should he?

The connection cut, he went to the laptop and waited. True to her word, she sent over the information immediately. He printed it off and set to working his way through it, looking for patterns, coincidences, and names cropping up again and again.

At just after noon, Lambert came into Beverley's office. He looked at the whiteboard which was set up at one end of the office between the two desks. "Dead? You think the bastard's dead?"

"It might not be high up on the list of possibilities, sir, but it shouldn't be ignored."

"We've got seven dead people now. Your prayers were answered, Bayes." He cast a withering look at the sergeant. "I expect you to make rapid progress towards a resolution now."

With which, and as if he had come in merely to mock their efforts, he snorted and left, giving his head a gentle shake. Beverley looked at Bayes, who was punching in the number of Emile Durkheim's old employers. She said nothing and he kept his gaze averted.

At six, she said, "Come on, to the pub, Bayes. That's an order."

"What about Frazier?"

"What about him?" She looked around the office. "Is he here?"

"He said he was going to get a coffee."

"That was an hour ago. The fucker's sneaked off home, I bet."

Bayes knew better than to argue with his superior. He stood up and fetched his coat from the rack by the door.

In the pub, she said to him over lagers, "Tell me about Adrian."

He looked at her and she thought it was almost with fear. Was her reputation that overwhelming? Perhaps it was. He said uncertainly, "He's a social worker."

"Really?" Like lawyers, they were so often the enemy, getting in the way, defending what seemed to her to be indefensible, allowing freedom for the obviously guilty. "I bet that leads to some interesting evenings."

"He's had cancer."

She had been taking a drink as he said this. "Oh, shit. I'm sorry, Tom . . ."

"He's in remission, though."

"That's good." She waited for him to take a mouthful of drink before taking one herself this time. "You live together?"

"Have done for three years."

"Married?"

He dropped his head. "Not yet." *But you want to be*, she guessed.

She said gently, "One day, perhaps."

He took a deep draught, which was something of a relief to her. Although he had a pint and she a half, he had until then hardly touched his. What was wrong with him? Why was he so buttoned up? But if she was feeling comfortable at last, his next question unsettled her completely. "What about John Eisenmenger?"

She put her glass down. "What about him?"

"You were close . . ."

She eyed him. He was, she judged, naïve. He shouldn't have asked such questions, not in his position. Yet he had, which made her think about things that she had hidden away, maybe unwisely. "We still are."

He looked at his glass, drew his finger through the condensation. "May I ask . . .?" He was going to ask no matter, so she remained wordless and just looked at him. "What you see in him?"

A good question.

Ask the right questions. That's the important thing . . .

She tried to analyse what it was about the pathologist that attracted her so much. At first, she had thought it was merely to take something from Helena Flemming, to best her, but Helena had been dead a long time now. "I wish I knew." She tried to laugh, but it was an ugly sound, even to her ears.

Bayes, though, didn't react as she had feared. He said gently, "It's a funny thing, love . . ."

Love? Surely, she didn't still love John Eisenmenger, did she? She felt a continuing attraction to him, true, but it wasn't love, was it?

Bayes asked then, "Is he as good a pathologist as you think he is?" It was an impertinent question but Sergeant Tom Bayes didn't seem to mind asking impertinent questions. Which was no bad thing in a copper, she realised.

She looked him directly in the eye. "Yes."

"And there's no one else in your life?"

She felt like telling him to fuck off. What business was it of his? Yet she found herself answering as if she were there for counselling. "Not at the moment."

He nodded, finished his drink, held the glass and looked at the foam as it tumbled down its interior surface. "I was told terrible things about you."

"I bet you were."

"I'm not so green as to believe everything that's said to me, though."

"If you're going to make a decent police officer, you'd better learn to disbelieve everything until you've seen the evidence . . ."

"I've seen no evidence concerning you, sir."

"It's 'Beverley' out of hours."

He looked at her, for a moment suspicious, then nodding. "Beverley, then," he said slowly, as if trying it in his mouth.

She laughed. "Another drink? One for the road?"

"Why not?"

As she went to the bar, she found herself deciding that maybe she could work with Tom Bayes, and that maybe he would make a decent copper.

Chapter Twenty-Four

Eisenmenger shook his head. He had known that it wouldn't be easy, but coordinating the arrivals of all of these patients in the Emergency Department together with the rotas of so many nursing, medical and ancillary staff was nigh on impossible. It didn't help that he wasn't completely convinced that there was anything actually to see; this doubt, he was sure, was having a detrimental effect on his efforts. He couldn't get it out of his head that Claire Woodforde was a bit of a loony; everyone told him so, so perhaps there was a germ of truth in it, which meant that perhaps he was chasing phantoms that existed only in her mind and nowhere else.

But he was driven to keep looking, if only to prove that she was wrong. But how do you prove a negative? That philosophical question kept nagging at him as he began once again to try to prove something, anything, from the information before him. Eisenmenger was well aware of the capacity for self-deception, which meant that perhaps he would see a pattern that wasn't actually there, that he would see what he wanted to see. Claire Woodforde's obsession verged on irrationality. Would he become infected?

Except that he knew that he was already infected with something else, something far more virulent, and something that he couldn't get out of his mind . . .

He stared at the screen for a while longer, then searched about for his mobile phone.

*

"What is it, John?" She was eager, he noted.

What was it? Now he was actually connected to her, he didn't know . . . Actually, that wasn't true. He *did* know, but he just didn't want to say.

He had to force himself to say, "I was wondering if I would be seeing you again . . ." Then, just to make sure that she fully appreciated what he was saying, he added unnecessarily, "Outside of work . . ."

"Oh . . ." No longer quite so eager, he noted. "Oh . . ."

"I take it that's a 'no'."

"I'm sorry, John."

He sighed. In truth, he told himself that he hadn't expected much more.

"We're rather busy, you know." He heard beautiful British understatement and saw what a dick he'd been and wondered why she'd felt the need to be defensive? He was only too aware of how busy she'd been. Christ, he'd had to do seven autopsies on torsos in varying states of decay, hadn't he? "I appreciate that, Beverley."

"Give me a call after the weekend; maybe we'll have more spare time."

"Won't I see you before then?"

She hesitated. He wondered why he had said anything, especially as his attention had been caught – perhaps it was *because* his attention had been caught – by her choice of words. '. . . maybe *we'll* . . . He felt oddly jealous of Bayes and wondered why. The feeling was magnified when she said, "I doubt it, John. We're up to our necks."

We, again. Why did that little pronoun bother him so much?

*

"Two matches on the DNA."

Bayes seemed barely able to control his excitement.

"Details, Sergeant. Who are they?"

"Samuel Kinison and Richard Warren."

"How come we've got their DNA profiles on record? What have they done?"

"Warren was done for drunk and disorderly. He had no fixed abode."

"Which one was he?"

Bayes looked through an on-screen file. "The second one from the bottom of the pile. Kinison was the one above him."

"The next one in, then." She turned to Eisenmenger's report on these two torsos. Warren's had been the body with putative scabies tracks. Kinison's had been well-nourished. "And Kinison?"

"Kinison gave an address in Lywych when he was charged with fraud. He used to be a solicitor, but was struck off when he was found guilty. Served three years."

"Married?"

"Divorced while he was in prison."

"Children?"

"None."

Kinison had had lung cancer, according to Eisenmenger's examination. Her father had had lung cancer. It had killed him and she had cursed God. Was she wrong?

"Nothing on the other four?"

"No." He looked at her, an expectant dog. "What shall I do?"

Last night, more of the details of the investigation had been released to the media. Beverley had called a press conference and, feeling like an idiot dummy, had explained that they now had seven bodies. The reaction had been typically hysterical, but she couldn't entirely blame them. There was a serial killer on the loose; who, if you worked for a newspaper or TV news company, wasn't going to enjoy frothing at the mouth at that one? Especially if, as was the case here, the police looked like incompetent duffers?

Can you give us any clue as to the killer's identity? No.

How many victims have you definitely identified? One.

How does the killer choose the victims? We're not sure.

The expression on Lambert's face as he stood at the back of the room – he had stayed out of the limelight – had been oddly confused. She guessed it had been an amalgam of pleasure at seeing her pilloried by the press pack and dismay that she had only told the truth; the police didn't know much.

*

But at least now they had two more identities to work with, and one of them had actually had an address. She went to the map, stuck a pin in Lywych. It formed a triangle with the other two pins; *of course* it formed a triangle. It meant nothing. She turned to Bayes.

"What do you think we should do?"

He didn't hesitate. "Go to Lywych. Ask around."

"Exactly."

*

"You're Superintendent Lambert, aren't you?"

Lambert had turned around as he was leaving the press conference, pleased to be recognised. He didn't know the woman before him. "That's right. And you are . . .?"

"Cordelia Hull. I work for the *Echo.*"

"Of course, of course . . ." He frowned. "What can I do for you?"

"Just a bit of background."

She smiled at him. Contrary to Beverley's opinion, he *did* have a heart and that smile did something to it. He asked, "What do you want to know?"

"The names of the team working on the case. I've obviously got yours and DCI Wharton's. Who's working under you?"

He saw no problem with that.

"Who's your pathologist?"

Why did she want to know that?

She ignored the question. "I was told it was John Eisenmenger. Is that true?"

"Who told you that?"

The smile had never left her face; now it broadened as she said, "So, it *is* true."

"It doesn't matter who the pathologist is."

"John Eisenmenger's got an interesting history, and we're always looking for a different angle, Superintendent."

*

Kinison's house was in fact a bungalow. It was large but had clearly not been lived in for a long time. The lawn at the front had grown in the spring rains, but not as much as the thistles and dandelions that now dominated it. There were weeds clearly to be seen amongst the shrubs in the borders and growing through the gravel of the drive. They rang the doorbell, not expecting an answer from within, not receiving one. There was one from a neighbour, though.

"It's empty."

An old man peered at them from the other side of the low fence. He was dressed in a tatty blue sweatshirt that had clearly seen far better days, and an old black beret. His face was tanned, his eyes were sharp, his lower lip hung down and trembled. Beverley walked over to him, Bayes following. She held up her warrant card. The man peered at it. "DCI Wharton. This is DS Bayes," she explained.

The old man asked, "What does that mean?"

"I'm Detective Chief Inspector Wharton; this is Detective Sergeant Bayes." She spoke gently.

The old man nodded. "Oh. The police."

"And you are?"

"George Beadle." His tone suggested, *You should have known that, being police.*

"How long has this place been empty, Mr Beadle?"

"Six, maybe seven months. He came out of prison – we knew what he'd done, of course – stayed here for a couple of months, and then just vanished. He wasn't a well man, when he came out, of course. I said to the wife, he's not a well man."

"He vanished, you say?"

"Yep. Vanished. Overnight."

"Did you see anyone else here at about the time he disappeared?"

"Nope. Can't say I did."

"What about your wife?"

"Nope."

"You're sure of that? Can we ask her?"

"You can when she gets back from shopping."

Bayes asked, "Who lives on the other side?" He looked over his shoulder as he said this.

"No one. This is the end of the street. It's just wood-land."

His tone was disdainful, as though everyone knew that and you were a moron if you didn't. Beverley found herself taking a dislike to him. She tried to keep this out of her voice as she enquired, "When will your wife be back home from her shopping?"

He shrugged. "Depends on whether she gets chatting."

"I suggest you go back inside your house and wait. Sergeant Bayes will be with you shortly."

"Why?"

"Because we'd like a statement."

"Why? What's that bastard gone and done now?" He indicated the bungalow behind them.

She shouldn't have said it, but she couldn't help herself. "He's gone and been murdered." The shocked expression on the old man's face was worth it, though. She suppressed a smile of satisfaction.

All the curtains were drawn, so that they couldn't see into any of the rooms, even the kitchen. Having carefully tracked around the bungalow, they opted to break in, which was harder to do than at first appeared. In the end, they broke down the back door using a lump hammer that Bayes found in the greenhouse at the end of a long garden. They found themselves in a sort of boot room with a rack for outdoor shoes, tatty and neat outdoor clothes, and a few wall cupboards.

And a stench . . .

Bayes looked at Beverley. She held his gaze for a moment before opening the door into the kitchen.

The stench became stronger.

She entered the kitchen and looked around. "Oh, shit," she whispered. Bayes came in behind her. "Oh, my God . . ."

The kitchen table was round and made of pine. It was laid for breakfast. Around it were four chairs, three of which were occupied by torsos.

Chapter Twenty-Five

"He has a sense of humour." Eisenmenger's tone was low and neutral.

"I got that."

"Did you see this?" He was crouching down between two of the torsos and pointing at the toast rack.

Bayes asked, "What is it?"

"A piece of paper. The only incongruous thing here. Otherwise, it's a perfect breakfast tableau."

Beverley picked the paper out with gloved hands. It was folded once. On it were three typed words: *MORE TEA, VICAR?*

She showed it to Bayes before handing it over to one of the Scenes of Crime Officers. Bayes asked, "What does it mean?"

Eisenmenger shrugged but didn't reply.

Bayes asked Beverley, "Is one of them a vicar? Is that what it means?"

Keith McCarthy

"Possibly."

"Wouldn't a vicar be missed?"

"Not necessarily. Not if he was 'between parishes'."

"If one of them's a Christian priest, maybe that's significant . . ." Beverley knew full well what her sergeant was talking about, and wasn't particularly pleased to hear it. She said angrily, "Why don't you check it out, then, Bayes? Do something useful."

He left but not before Eisenmenger saw hurt on his face. Before he could comment, she asked, "What are those marks? They're not like the spots on the first torso. And they're on all three torsos."

But Eisenmenger was Eisenmenger and he recounted his observations and deductions without regard to her question. "They're all male again. Decaying but noticeably more recent than the bodies in the shed."

"How old?"

"This one . . ." he pointed at the one nearest the window, ". . . is less than two weeks old, I'd say." He walked around and stood behind another of the torsos. "This one has probably been dead five to six weeks. The third is older; perhaps nine or ten weeks."

She wrote this down and he added, "All this is very approximate, of course."

She raised her eyes and looked at him. "Of course."

He ignored her, or perhaps didn't hear her. "They have varying nutritional states." He smiled humourlessly, "More evidence that he's running out of vagrants, perhaps."

"And perhaps one's a vicar, given the note."

"You don't believe that."

She shook her head. "No. That note was left to confuse us, I think. That said . . ."

"You can't afford to ignore it?"

"No, we can't. The usual signs of torture, I see."

"Cuts and burns on all three."

"Any signs that any of the limbs were removed whilst still living?"

"Not that I can see. Not the limbs, anyway. I would say that they were all beheaded while still alive, though."

"Which was the cause of death?"

"Probably."

"This is becoming boring."

"You think?" His voice was sad.

She read the warning signals. "What?"

"If I didn't know better, I'd say that the marks you asked about – on all three, note – were acid splashes."

Which made her pause. "Whilst they were still alive?"

"I'd say so."

"More torture."

"Looks like it."

She took a very deep breath. "Okay. Any other thoughts?"

He stood up. "Have you noticed how little blood there is on the floor?"

She looked down. He was right. "Significance?" she asked.

"Not much. It's interesting, though, suggesting that the corpses weren't put in place immediately."

"Any evidence that they were hung?" They were, after all, just carcasses.

"No marks suggestive of a hook, if that's what you mean." He was peeling off his gloves. She did likewise as they went out of the kitchen, through the boot room and thence into the garden where they both took lungfuls of fresh air.

She said, "You wouldn't say that there was a terrorist connection to this, would you, John?"

The question caught him by surprise. "Terrorist?"

"You know, beheadings . . . a reference to a vicar."

"Oh . . ."

"It's not my theory, but I thought I'd better ask."

"I wouldn't have thought so, Beverley. The rest of it all adds up to a common or garden lunatic to me." He smiled weakly. "The secular kind."

She smiled back, equally weakly. "That's something, I suppose." Then after a period of contemplation, "Why's the killer stopped removing limbs while they're still alive, John?"

"Too much like hard work, I'd say. When you can cut and burn and drop acid on them, why exert yourself amputating limbs?"

She shivered, and he wondered if it was due to the killer's sadism or his own apparent empathy with it. He said, "I'll know more after the post-mortems."

But, in the meantime, he had another matter to consider. He called Claire Woodforde's mobile as soon as he got home, but it went to voicemail. He left a message asking her to call back, which she did a couple of hours later.

"I need to see you, Claire."

"You've got something?"

"An oddity I need to discuss with you."

"When can we meet?"

His time was pretty much his own. "Whenever you like."

"I should be free at six. Can you come to my house at seven?"

He looked at his watch. Three o'clock. The post-mortems on the three newest torsos wouldn't take place until tomorrow. He tried to ignore her fevered eagerness. "See you then."

*

Lambert entered her office like a madman.

"Have you seen these?" He brandished newspapers. Lots of them. "And have you seen what's happening on the internet?"

In truth, she hadn't, but only because she could guess what was being said. After all, there were ten bodies . . .

"Ten bodies." Lambert thundered, slapping the papers down her desk. "*Ten.*"

"I can count."

"What?" He was incredulous.

She moderated her tone and added a word. "I can count, sir."

"And what progress have you made?"

"We've identified three of them. Two were down-and-outs, one was a disgraced solicitor."

"Three out of ten. Not many, is it?"

"Given all the factors . . ."

"I know, I know. No heads and no fingerprints."

"And putrefaction . . ."

"I'm coming under pressure, Wharton." She'd guessed that, since he was pressurising her. He was nothing more than a conduit, a large-calibre pipe, with a grand title. "The media can't understand why we haven't identified more."

"I told the press conference that the degree of decay would make things difficult."

"The chief constable was wondering if you'd brought in a forensic psychologist."

"For what?"

He didn't hide his anger. "To profile the killer. At the moment, you've got no idea who's doing this."

She knew exactly what the profile would say. She could quote it now. *The protagonist is a white male, of lower social class, who has malignant narcissist tendencies. He is most probably a functioning psychopath . . .*

She didn't need some poncey academic telling her what she already knew. The problem with such profiles was that they didn't help in any way to catch the killer. To do that, you needed police work, the old-fashioned kind, and lots of it. Which preferably meant lots of bodies helping out. And she only had Bayes and Frazier. She knew why, too;

because Superintendent Lambert wasn't about to commit a large amount of scarce resource to a case in which the only proven dead were criminals and vagrants.

"I'm not sure that it would help."

"I don't care, Wharton. The question's been asked. Get one."

Chapter Twenty-Six

Eisenmenger waited outside the large townhouse having rung the doorbell. There was no front garden and he stood on the pavement, but there were passers-by. It wasn't Claire who came to the door but her husband. He plumbed the depths of his memory for the man's name – Geoff? Gary? Justin? There had been so many names to remember from that night and his mind had been filled with other things since.

"John. Claire said you'd be calling. She's been delayed at the infirmary, I'm afraid. Come in, though, and wait. She shouldn't be long."

"Thanks."

He was tall and cadaverous. Not like a publisher at all, in Eisenmenger's opinion. He led the way into the house, through the cluttered hallway and into an equally cluttered kitchen. What was the bloody man's name? Jake? Joshua?

"Coffee? I've just made some." He waved a percolator around.

"Great."

"Sit down." He indicated one of three stools that were partially sheltering beneath the lea of a breakfast bar. He brought two white bone china cups with saucers to the bar and then filled them with coffee. "Milk? Sugar?"

"Just milk." Eisenmenger had done as ordered and was seated on one of the stools. When Claire's husband returned from the fridge with a litre carton of semi-skimmed milk, Eisenmenger appreciated for the first time that something more than hospitality was going on. The carton was put between the coffee cups.

"Help yourself."

Eisenmenger did so as the other sat opposite him. "How long do you think she'll be?" he asked.

A shrug. "It was some emergency on the unit. She's not on call, but . . ."

Eisenmenger said carefully, "It can't be easy, being married to an intensivist."

"No."

"You're a publisher, aren't you? What kind?"

The other had taken a large drink of black coffee. "Children's books." He grimaced. "Ironic, really . . ."

"I don't understand." And Eisenmenger genuinely didn't.

"We can't have them, you see. Children . . ."

"Oh . . ." Eisenmenger felt like an obtuse fool. This house was an adult's abode, and he should have worked it out, or at least had an inkling about the truth of the situation here.

The other blurted out, "It's my fault. Low sperm count." John Eisenmenger really didn't want to know about that. Worse was to come, though. "I think it's why she's always having affairs."

He didn't know what to say. There was nothing he *could* say. He opened his mouth as a sort of substitute for responding verbally, perhaps to show that words were failing him. What *was* his name? It came to him quite abruptly, but the confession hadn't ended. "It's relatively easy for her, what with nights on call."

"Look, Matthew . . ."

The man looked up from his now empty coffee cup. So well made and expensive, so refined, so First World; he spoke of a situation that cut across geography and aeons, though. He stared directly at Eisenmenger. "It was Sulston for a while. Now, I think it's someone else. I'm not sure who, though . . ."

His gaze pinned Eisenmenger. He surely didn't think it was him, did he? He didn't get the chance to protest his innocence. Still staring at him, Matthew went on, "I tell myself it's displacement activity. Like this business about a killer being on the loose in the hospital."

"You don't believe it?"

"Do you?" It sounded remarkably like a challenge.

"I didn't . . ."

"But you do now? You've discovered something?" The publisher sounded partly incredulous, partly eager.

The phone rang. It was on the windowsill to Matthew's right, Eisenmenger's left. Matthew looked at it for a while, as if he already knew what the call would be about, that it would bring only more sadness; then he rose and went to it. "Yes?"

Eisenmenger saw him close his eyes as someone spoke to him. "Okay. I'll tell him. Take care."

He put the phone down and turned to Eisenmenger. "That was Claire. She won't be able to get away for several hours. She asked me to apologise to you."

He sounded to Eisenmenger's ears as if he didn't believe it, and cared only a little.

"I'd better go, then." Eisenmenger got off the stool.

"She said she'd be in contact tomorrow."

"Fine."

Eisenmenger was led through the hall. At the door, Matthew turned and smiled without warmth. "I'm really very sorry."

"No problem."

The front door was opened and Eisenmenger ushered out. He walked away slowly and the noise of the door closing came from behind him; he tried to shake off the melancholy that had settled upon him in that house, as if the coffee had been adulterated with liquid sadness.

When he got home, Eisenmenger thought about working again on Claire Woodforde's case but he was now totally confused. Matthew had been convinced that his wife was pursuing a fantasy, and he had been told repeatedly by various persons in the days before that Claire was not operating with all her cylinders firing in sequence. Yet he thought he had found something. It was by far from enough to convict anyone, but there was a definite common thread that ran through all the cases that she had identified.

Was it the answer?

More to the point, was it the answer that she wanted?

Exactly to the point, was it an answer to anything? Couldn't it just be a pattern that he saw because he was desperate to see such things? Animals in the clouds, faces in the wallpaper patterns, odd pictures in the raindrops on the outside of the window on a winter's day.

The notebook remained where he had put it when he had tried to convince Beverley that it was worth a small piece of her time to join him in his – and Claire's – beliefs. He left it there and went to bed.

He missed the piece that led the *Echo* that night. The headline read, "*TORSO CASE CONTINUES TO BAFFLE POLICE*". It included his name as the pathologist who was working with the police and, deeper inside the paper, his potted biography, including the pertinent facts that he lived alone and was unattached.

Chapter Twenty-Seven

The whiteboard now included reference to Samuel Kinison and Richard Warren. Lee Frazier and his hygiene problems sat behind his desk. Bayes sat on the front of Beverley's as she stood in front of the whiteboard, but leaned away from him, perhaps unconsciously, Beverley thought. She couldn't blame him. She asked, "What do we know today that we didn't know yesterday?" She held today a blue marker pen.

Frazier was apparently keen to show that he wasn't just a slob with BO. "Warren had done time."

"When? How long?"

Frazier flipped through his notebook. "He was in Moorland for four months, at the end of last year."

Bayes asked, "Moorland? Yorkshire?"

Frazier nodded. He had a round face that was still erupting with acne, despite his age of over thirty.

Beverley picked up on Bayes' excitement. "What of it?" she asked.

"Kinison was there just prior to transfer to Hatfield."

"At the same time as Warren?"

"From September last year until January this year."

Beverley smiled. "So, that's a 'yes' then." She turned to the whiteboard and connected the two names with an arrow; along the arrow, she wrote "*Moorlands*".

Frazier asked, "How big is Moorlands?"

Bayes, of course, had the information in his head. "About a thousand prisoners."

"So, big enough that they might never have met."

Beverley had been staring at the whiteboard, her arms folded, the marker pen held between the forefinger and middle finger of her left hand. She turned around to face Frazier. "Find out, then." She looked at her watch. "We need to get to the mortuary."

*

Eisenmenger had left his small house fifteen minutes before, aware that he was late and therefore hurrying. He walked quickly to the end of the mews, looked right and left, saw nothing coming and stepped into the road. The car that hit him must have come out of nowhere. Having hit him, it disappeared into the same place and he was left sprawled on the tarmac, bleeding from an abrasion on his left temple and feeling intense pain in his chest and right knee. He was concussed, with the world whirling around him. He smelled the tarmac and heard nothing except an internal screaming in his skull.

Chapter Twenty-Eight

"Where the hell has he got to? It's not like him."

White had just returned to the dissection room. "There's no answer either from his mobile phone or his landline." He made his way between the three sealed body bags. His tone had been oddly triumphant, as if he had just won an argument. He walked with the air of a man who was king in his own domain. Beverley guessed that he saw this as a victory, perhaps because of some sort of rivalry between technician and pathologist.

She decided, "Something must have happened to him."

White snorted but said nothing.

Bayes asked, "What do we do?"

She was already walking out. "Find him."

White looked at Bayes. "What shall *I* do?"

"You wait."

He, too, walked out before White could reply.

Eisenmenger returned to full consciousness in the Emergency Department with a brace around his neck, his right leg splinted, intravenous drips inserted into the back of each hand, and a thumping headache. A nurse dressed in dark green scrubs and wearing disposable gloves was applying steri-strips to his temple with fine forceps; she appeared to be upside down as she came into unfocused view. He said groggily, "Hello."

He saw a tight smile as she leaned away from him and into focus. "Hello."

"What happened?" God, his chest hurt. He felt that he couldn't breathe properly and it was a scary feeling.

"You're a hit and run," she replied, as if he were that which had been done to him. He frowned, and it hurt. She said sternly, "Don't do that. You'll make it bleed again."

He smelled flowers and couldn't tell whether it was her perfume, disinfectant or an olfactory hallucination. He felt like shit. He hurt all over. He couldn't remember anything clearly; he could hardly remember anything at all. The nurse leaned forward again and his view of her blurred. He felt her working again at his temple with the cold metal of the forceps for a few moments, before she again straightened up. "There."

He involuntarily took a deep breath, regretting it immediately. "Fuck!"

She looked anything but shocked as she said, "Language, please, doctor."

"I was in agony." The room began to spin. Slowly, but it was definitely moving. He thought this odd.

She stood up from her stool. "So I gathered," she said as she pushed a small stainless steel trolley to one side of what he now saw was a large alcove painted in pale orange and closed off along one side with a green curtain. He became aware of a hum of conversation and movement coming from the other side of this, but it echoed. The nurse pulled off her gloves and threw them onto the trolley where it joined a kidney bowel filled with water, three bloody cotton swabs, some discarded wrappings and the forceps. She grasped the side of the curtain and ducked through, pulling the trolley after her.

Eisenmenger raised his head, only to lower it again because of the intense pain in his neck and because the movement made the spinning of the world around him worse. He had to content himself with looking at the ceiling as he called to her, "Thank you." He couldn't stop his voice slurring.

Her reply came back to him from the either side of the curtain. "You're welcome." It was moving away.

He had to wait, he knew not how long, before something else happened. The curtain was drawn aside and he heard Peter Sulston's voice. "As I live and breathe, it's Doctor John Eisenmenger!" He came into the alcove, drawing the curtain behind him. "Been playing with the traffic, I hear."

"Apparently. I don't remember much about it."

Sulston came into his purview. He had a tablet computer in one hand, but his eyes were on Eisenmenger. "How are you, John?"

"Everything hurts." He was fed up with lying flat on his back.

"Collisions with cars will do that."

"Have I got broken ribs?"

"Clinically, yes."

"How many?"

"At least two on the right. We'll know for sure when you go for a chest x-ray."

"And what's wrong with my knee?"

"Just bruised, I think. What really concern me are your head and neck. You've had a serious head injury. You lost consciousness for a while, and now you sound as if you've had half a dozen pints."

"My head and my neck generally concern me quite a lot as well. Is there any possibility of propping me up a bit? The ceiling's becoming quite boring."

Sulston ignored his request and Eisenmenger had the feeling that the other, at least, was enjoying the situation. "We'll need a CT scan to make sure there isn't an extradural bleed . . ." He checked the tablet, tapped on it with a stylus he produced from the top pocket of his scrubs. "Your bloods are okay, anyway."

"You sound disappointed."

Sulston looked down at him. "What are you talking about?"

Ignoring the question, Eisenmenger asked, "Assuming that I don't show signs of an intracranial bleed, can I go home?"

Sulston grimaced. "You know better than that. You're not thinking straight and that's because you're concussed. You're going to stay in and you'll be on four-hourly neuro observations while you're in our care. If you're okay tomorrow morning, then you can go home."

Eisenmenger had known that would be the answer. Sulston went to the curtain. "I'm afraid we're very busy. It might be some time, but at least you've got visitors to pass the time."

With which he passed through the curtain and Eisenmenger heard him say, "You can see him now."

Beverley and Bayes entered the alcove. Eisenmenger was well past caring who came in and who didn't. He speculated that it might be the concussion, then speculated that he didn't give a toss; he was in too much pain. The spinning of all around him was becoming tedious. "Hello, John." she said. "We need to talk to you."

The brace was chafing the skin under his chin. The venous drips going into his hands were beginning to bother him. The abrasion on his temple was throbbing; his knee felt as if it were being pumped full of something warm and viscid and acidic. Every time he breathed, it hurt; his head ached abominably. And he wanted to go home, but knew that he couldn't.

"Can't it wait?" he said irritably, refusing to look at her.

"No, it can't." He knew from old that she could be stubborn. It was born, he supposed, from nature, and nurture as a police officer.

"Prop me up, then. It's the least you can do if you're going to interrogate me."

Bayes crouched down and fiddled at the side of Eisenmenger's trolley. Suddenly the upper half of Eisenmenger's body began to rise; his initial elation turned quickly to dismay as intense pain shot through his right side. "Stop!" he nearly screamed.

Beverley came at once to his side. "What's wrong?"

"My ribs . . . Shit, that hurts . . ." He rolled his head. "Lower me a bit . . . Please . . ."

Bayes complied and Eisenmenger breathed a little more easily, thinking to himself that perhaps Peter Sulston had earlier been doing him a favour. "Better?" asked Bayes.

Eisenmenger nodded. "Yes, thanks."

Beverley held his hand. "Sure?"

He felt much better, he decided. He nodded again, this time with a smile for her. He asked, "What can I do for you?"

"Tell us what happened."

*

"You're not being a lot of help."

"I didn't think I would be. Retrograde amnesia. It's very common after significant trauma, Beverley."

"Yeah, I know, but it's still fucking annoying."

"Sorry." He started to shrug but the pain in his side stopped him quickly. His head throbbed.

"Are you sure you'll be able to carry on with the case?"

"Don't worry, if they let me out tomorrow, I'll be there at the mortuary as soon as I can."

Bayes had shut his notebook a while ago. Beverley gestured with her head that he should leave. When he had gone, she bent down and kissed John Eisenmenger. "Take care, John," she said softly. "Give me a call when you're due to get out of here. I'll come and pick you up."

As they walked away, Bayes said to her, "Do you think it was connected with the torso case?"

"Possibly."

"To stop him doing the autopsies?"

"I doubt it. Pathologists are ten a penny."

"I thought you were of the opinion that he was somehow special."

"You said it yourself, Bayes. That's just my opinion."

"So maybe it's *not* connected to the case."

"Maybe. I'm not sure. It could be just a random event. Who knows?"

"What do we do then?"

She sighed. "I'll pick him up tomorrow. In the meantime, he'll be safe in here."

"And after that?"

"I haven't thought that far ahead, Bayes. I'll let you know when *I* know."

Chapter Twenty-Nine

The porter who pushed Eisenmenger to the Radiology Department was the same one he had met the last time he had been in the hospital, although the porter didn't seem to remember. He chatted interminably as he pushed him along, a nurse at the other end of the bed, making little attempt to pull.

"Are you the Eisenmenger that was mentioned in the papers?" he asked.

"I don't know."

"You a pathologist?"

"What of it?"

"You've been involved with all those murdered tramps?"

The nurse turned, her interest piqued. "I heard about those. Who would do such a thing?"

Eisenmenger was looking at the ceiling. The porter remained silent on the point.

The nurse said with absolute certainty, "A madman, that's who."

The porter asked, "You reckon?"

"All serial killers are mad."

The porter shook his head. "I'm not so sure."

"Of course, they are," insisted the nurse.

Eisenmenger now felt totally forgotten as the conversation continued between the nurse and the porter; the nurse was the one who had applied steri-strips to Eisenmenger's temple. He lifted his head as far as he could; she appeared quite attractive, he thought. The porter had an idiot grin on his face, one which Eisenmenger knew well: the porter had taken advantage of the situation and was attempting to chat her up. Eisenmenger looked back at the nurse. Although she appeared to engage in the banter, he suspected that this was a tactic to remain aloof, for he detected artifice in her demeanour.

The nurse asked, "How many murders is it now?"

Eisenmenger said dreamily, "Seven."

"God . . ."

Eisenmenger said, "Don't worry. I'll get him." In truth, his attention was wandering. The room's spinning was so distracting.

"You will?"

"We will, I meant."

The porter asked, "Play an important role, do you? As a pathologist, I mean."

Eisenmenger had spent his whole life trying to persuade

anyone who would listen how important pathology was. "Of course."

In the waiting area of the Radiology Department, Eisenmenger and the nurse – whom he could now see from her name badge was called Jody Williams – were about to be left alone by the porter when she said suddenly, "I need the loo. Look after him, will you?"

With which she was hurrying away. The porter said, "Oh . . ." He spoke into his walkie-talkie. "This is Paul. I've been delayed in radiology. I'll let you know when I'm free."

Eisenmenger heard static; apparently the porter heard something intelligible, for he said, "Will do."

He bent down beside Eisenmenger. "Fucking women."

Eisenmenger laughed, although he didn't feel like it. He closed his eyes and drifted off into discomforted sleep . . .

"What's wrong?" Jody Williams' voice jerked him awake.

The porter had something in his hand, was fiddling with the drip. He said, "Oh, sorry . . ."

"Is there something wrong with the drip?"

"It wasn't running properly."

"Let me see."

"I've fixed it."

A pause as she came and looked to the drip that was running into Eisenmenger's right hand. The porter stood back. Eisenmenger thought that perhaps he put something in his pocket. They made brief eye contact. The nurse said, "It *looks* all right."

"I told you I fixed it."

"Well . . . You can go now. I'm back."

There was a burst of static. "Paul here. I've finished in radiology."

Eisenmenger was in a draught but he didn't have the courage to tell Jody. In fact, they said nothing more to each other as they waited. People came in and people left, some into the depths of the department accompanied by radiographers, some in the opposite direction through the exit doors to the main hospital corridor. Eventually, it was Eisenmenger's turn when a grey-haired radiographer of about fifty came out through a door behind his head and said to Nurse Williams, "John Eisenmenger?" She said that yes, it was, leaving Eisenmenger to feel that here was the final proof that he had been totally swallowed by the medical machine.

The radiographer had a tablet computer and he came around to Eisenmenger's left side so that he could compare information on its screen with his hospital bracelet. He was dressed in blue. He said nothing to Eisenmenger, as if he thought the patient mute. Eisenmenger felt too shitty to argue. The radiographer grunted, raised his head, nodded at Jody Williams, and then moved again out of Eisenmenger's line of sight. The trolley began to move into the depths of the Radiology Department.

After the chest x-ray and the CT scan of his head,

Eisenmenger was taken to a ward where he passed the night without proper rest. Part of the problem was the four-hourly neurological observations that were done to him; part of the problem was the other patients on the ward, who coughed, and shouted, and sighed, and talked, and gabbled, and . . .

The light of the morning came slowly but Eisenmenger was grateful to see it, and with it came a cup of tea that was disgusting but wet and warm and therefore welcome. The men around him who had coughed and shouted and . . . also drank the same peculiarly disgusting brew and, oddly, a camaraderie was formed between them on that ward.

Peter Sulston came to see him after a breakfast that consisted of Weetabix, a banana, semi-skimmed milk and some more disgusting tea. He said, "You can go home."

"No intracranial bleed?"

"No."

"What about the rib fractures?"

"We'll give you some painkillers."

"Strong painkillers."

He frowned. "Something with codeine in, I should think. Will that do you?"

Eisenmenger dressed with difficulty behind curtains. Around him he heard the sounds of the ward as it moved from early morning until lunch, pleased that he would not be a part of it for much longer. He rang Beverley, but got no answer. His TTOs arrived. He called Beverley again, but still she didn't answer. He left the ward having said nothing either to his fellow patients or to the nurses whom he'd hardly spoken to. He was limping, his head still ached and he could only take shallow breaths which left him feeling light-headed and only just on the right side of fainting.

He bumped into the porter in the corridor.

"You okay? You don't look it."

"Don't I? Apparently I'm fit for discharge."

The porter laughed. "You wait here. I'll get you a chair and push you to the main foyer, if you like."

"That would be very kind. Thank you."

The porter soon reappeared with a wheelchair. Eisenmenger climbed gratefully in, clutching the paper bag with his drugs in; he had nothing else, save for his mobile and wallet. As the porter pushed him, he said, "How you going to get home?"

"I was hoping for a lift from a friend, but she's not answering. I suppose I'd better get a taxi."

"Try this firm." The porter produced a card and held it in front of Eisenmenger, who took it. *Dunant Taxis.* "They're the cheapest."

Eisenmenger began to laugh, finding quickly that it a hurt a great deal. "Do you get commission?"

The porter laughed too. "I wish . . ."

In the hospital foyer, the porter left him. Eisenmenger had a flat white from the coffee shop. Whilst he was drinking it, he tried Beverley one more time, this time leaving a

163

voicemail. He looked at the card, shrugged and phoned the number on it. The taxi arrived five minutes later and he got in.

"You were quick."

The driver turned and smiled. He was very neat and tidy, Eisenmenger thought. "I was in the area."

Chapter Thirty

The park was a scrappy affair, and generally only attracted people who, Beverley felt, were also scrappy. The call had come through fifteen minutes before, conveyed by Frazier with great excitement. "They've found an arm!"

"Where?" asked Bayes.

"Gloucester Park."

"Where in Gloucester Park?" asked Beverley.

"In a waste bin."

Beverley found a degree of inevitability about this. She stood up. "Let's go and see."

Bayes stood also, then stopped suddenly. "What about Eisenmenger?"

Yes, good question. She had been worrying about him all morning. He hadn't called. She checked her phone. The battery was dead. "Shit . . ."

"Problem?"

"Give me your phone, Bayes."

He raised his eyebrows but complied. As they hurried from the office and down the corridor of the station, she called Eisenmenger's phone but he didn't answer. She called his home; again, no answer. Frowning, she phoned the infirmary. It took a frustratingly long time to locate the ward where he had spent the night. She was told that he had been discharged over an hour ago. She cut the connection and handed the phone back to Bayes. "He'll have to wait."

*

The waste bin was towards one side of the park, near the children's playground, not far from the main road; a large Kentucky Fried Chicken drive-through was opposite, and there was a smell of car exhaust drifting over the abundant litter that blew around them. An ambulance was parked nearby. The bin was next to a bench, just off a tarmac pathway that led from the pavement next to the main road into the heart of the park. A square area about twenty metres along each side was cordoned off with yellow-and-black police tape; the bench and the bin were at its centre, surrounded by four crime scene investigation officers, all in bodysuits.

"Close to the road," was Beverley's initial comment.

"Easy to drop off, you mean?"

"Exactly."

The perimeter was being patrolled by four uniforms, one

to each side. Phelps was there, acknowledging them with a nod. He, Beverley and Bayes ducked under the tape and headed for the bin. "Who found it?" she asked as they walked towards the bin.

"A young mother. Miss Emily Batch. She's in the ambulance."

"What was she doing rummaging around in a waste bin?"

Phelps smiled grimly. "She saw someone put something large in the bin. Curiosity got the better of her."

Beverley stopped abruptly. "You mean . . .?"

Phelps nodded. "She saw our man."

It was a sorry thing. Severely charred, and wrapped badly in a large, white plastic bag, it wouldn't have escaped attention for long, Beverley guessed. The fingers were still plainly visible as she peered down at it. Keeping her hands in her pockets, she asked one of the crime scene officers, "Anything?"

The officer shook her head.

"Has anyone taken it out of the bin yet?"

Another shake of the auburn hair.

"Do it, would you?"

Bayes and Phelps came forward as the arm was removed. The fingers poked out, although the thumb wasn't visible. Bayes asked, "Has the thumb been removed?"

"Looks like it."

They exchanged looks; they knew what that meant. *Torture.*

The crime scene officer was looking closely at the fingers

as she held the arm in gloved hands. It was heavily charred, largely down to bone. "There's a ring," she said. Her voice was full of wonder, as if she couldn't quite believe it. "A signet ring."

They talked to Emily Batch in her flat, trying to ignore the smell of sick and dirty nappies; at least, Beverley thought, the slight odour of damp that pervaded the small flat did something to mask the stench. All around them was chaos, with every surface covered by something, many of which were baby related, many of which were just rubbish. There was a huge number of empty pizza boxes, burger trays and drinks cans. Emily was large but had the dress sense of a size zero; a blindness that seemed to Beverley had become distressingly prevalent in modern society. Her muffin top had a life of its own, wobbling at random and, disturbingly, apparently sometimes with purpose. She had too much make-up on for Beverley's taste but she saw that Bayes didn't seem to mind, and Emily Batch didn't seem to mind that he didn't mind. Beverley caught his eye and she could see that he guessed what she was thinking, for he looked down quickly.

"You're on your own, Emily?" Bayes asked after room had been made for them on the stained sofa by the simple expedient of removing empty food boxes. Beverley had suggested that he should take the lead.

"My choice," she replied defensively. She sat drinking a coke that Beverley had seen her put rum into. Her voice was still shaking.

"What have you got?"

"A little boy."

"What's his name?"

"Dean."

"Nice name," he opined. Beverley thought it hideous. "Where is he?"

"Mum's got him."

He nodded. Beverley wondered how often Dean spent time with his grandmother, deciding that it was probably *a lot*.

"Can you tell us what happened, Emily?"

She shrugged, took a large drink of coke. "I found . . ."

"We know what you found, Emily," he interrupted. "There's no need to relive that." Beverley was impressed. Bayes said, "You saw who left it there? Is that right?"

"I saw a bloke leave something there . . ." She took another drink and emptied the glass. "I'm thirsty." She waggled the glass at them. "Do you mind if I get some more coke?"

Bayes said, "Of course not."

She waddled out without offering anything to her guests. Beverley lay back on the sofa trying not to think of the stains or how uncomfortable it was. She murmured, "I hope she's got enough rum."

Bayes whispered in reply, "The more the merrier."

She smiled. Emily returned, her glass full of "coke", and sat back down.

"Can you describe him? The man who left it in the bin?"

"Not really."

Open questions never worked when trying for a description; the more closed the better, in fact.

"Was he tall or short?"

"Short, I think."

"What colour was his hair? Was he fair-haired, or dark, or a ginger?"

She thought, or appeared to do so. "Fair, I think." But this was uncertain. Bayes noted it anyway.

"How old, would you say?"

"Oh, young."

"How young? In his twenties? Thirties? Older?"

"In his twenties, I'd have said."

"What were you doing when you saw him?"

She frowned. "Why?"

Bayes explained patiently, "I'm just trying to get a picture of the scene. Where were you?"

"Sitting on a swing." She sounded embarrassed.

"With Dean?"

"I told you, Dean's with his granny."

"But you were in the children's playground?"

She dropped her eyes to the bright red carpet that didn't look as though it had been hoovered for months. "That's right."

"Doing what?"

"Having a smoke." There was something about the way she said it that suggested to Beverley that it hadn't been tobacco that she was smoking, but neither she nor Bayes cared.

"And that's when you saw this man?"

"Yeah."

"Which direction did he come from?"

Her expression suggested that this was a stupid question. "From the road, of course."

"Why do you say 'of course'?" Beverley was impressed with Bayes' patience.

"Because he got out of the taxi that had stopped."

"A taxi?" This was the first time that either of them had heard this particular snippet.

Beverley leaned forward. She asked, "He had taken a taxi?"

But she shook her head. "No."

"No?" Neither of them understood. "I don't understand. You said he got out of a taxi."

"That's right, but he hadn't taken it. He was the driver."

Chapter Thirty-One

Beverley looked at the map. Frazier had dutifully put another pin into it and now an irregular rectangular shape had been formed. The centre of it was in the heart of the city. Was that significant? Kenilworth Avenue, or somewhere around there. She shook her head, aware that it was all too easy to see patterns that weren't there. What was it that John said? *The whole of the evolution of the human central nervous system had been to discern patterns in the wilderness. It's very good at it. Perhaps sometimes too good.*

Or some shit like that.

And where was he? She had now recharged her phone and called both his mobile and landline without direct result, except for the voicemail:

Hi, Beverley,

Don't know what the problem is, but I'm going to get a taxi home. Call me there.

And she thought, *A taxi . . . Surely not . . .*

She needed him for the autopsies on the three torsos found at Lywych, and now a pathologist's opinion on the arm found in the park. And he'd vanished off the radar, shortly after taking a taxi ride. And the limb had been left by a taxi driver.

Bayes came in. "The signet ring had an inscription."

"Saying what?"

"*With Love To Mervyn.*"

It was a beautifully uncommon name. "Does it match . . .?"

But Bayes was ahead of her. "Mervyn Bridgeman, went missing eight weeks ago."

"A vagrant? An ex-con?"

"Neither."

"But he lived alone . . .?"

"He did, in Churchdown. He was forty-six years old but retired, and had never married."

"Who reported him missing?"

"His sister, Cara Lamb." Bayes was reading this off a screen. "She was also his carer."

"His carer?"

"He had learning difficulties. The ring was a gift from her."

"We'd better talk to her. Where does she live?"

"Also in Churchdown."

Before they left, she tried to call Eisenmenger again, but again without success.

*

"Is that the ring you gave to your brother?"

Cara was apparently forty-nine but looked nearer sixty. Perhaps it was the tears. Her husband, Greg, sat next to her; they sat with fingers intertwined, and he looked almost as worried as she did. She nodded, blubbing loudly. "Where did you get it?" she asked, but only on the fifth attempt could she complete the question.

Beverley said as gently as she could, "We think your brother may be dead, Mrs Lamb. We won't know for certain until . . . some more tests are done, but I think you should prepare yourself for bad news." Which precipitated another flood of tears, this time accompanied by an embrace from Mr Lamb.

"Oh, my God!"

Beverley looked around the room. It was nicely furnished and clean, if a little fussy for her taste. Still, it was good not to have to feel dirty, just being in a space. She came back to Mrs Lamb. "Tell me about Mervyn. He had learning difficulties, I understand."

A nod.

"But he lived independently?"

Another nod.

"Close by?"

"Just around the corner." A huge sniff. The handholding was now tight, Beverley noted; she could see that the flesh of both their hands was white around the pressure points.

"And he disappeared about eight weeks ago. Is that right?"

"Yes. Yes."

Bayes asked, "How much did you do for Mervyn?"

"I used to clean and tidy for him. And I did his washing every week."

"And we did his shopping, don't forget."

Beverley saw with interest that Mrs Lamb seemed to resent her husband's interjection.

"Yes, that too."

"He was retired, is that right? What did he used to do?"

"He was a warehouse operative."

What the fuck does that mean? Beverley and Bayes exchanged covert glances but, before they could seek clarification, Mrs Lamb said, "He took early retirement."

"Why?"

But she was overcome and her husband had to explain, "He wasn't well."

"Oh?"

"His heart, or something." He shook his head. "I never quite got the hang of it."

Mrs Lamb added through tears, "Unstable angina. He was under a cardiologist and it was him who recommended that Mervyn should stop work."

"You made a report when he went missing, I see," Beverley was recapping things that she knew well; she also knew well that the more times people recounted their stories, the more they tended to remember. "Can you take us through the last time you saw him?"

She had to think hard, Beverley saw and wondered why. "I'd done his washing, like always . . ."

"What day was that?"

"Wednesday. I always did his washing on a Wednesday."

Beverley asked, "Did you see him when you picked it up?" A nod. "What day was that?"

"Monday."

"So that was the last time you saw him?"

"That's right."

"You didn't phone each other or anything like that?"

She shook her head. "It's only just around the corner, you see. I don't . . . didn't . . . want him to think that we were looking after him."

"He treasured his independence?"

"It was very important to him."

"Do you know what he had planned for the Monday, and Tuesday?"

"He had a hospital appointment on the Tuesday."

Which, Beverley already knew, he had attended without incident.

Bayes asked, "How did he get there and back?"

"By taxi."

"What firm?"

She looked at her husband. He shrugged. She said to Bayes, "We don't know. Is it important?"

*

Lambert simmered. Beverley was well used to this, but she saw that it was having a bad effect on Bayes. Frazier didn't seem bothered, but then the big fat slob wouldn't have been bothered by the sound of the Last Trump breaking the windows of the meeting room where they now sat. The map and whiteboard had been moved in there and Lambert was examining these wordlessly.

"It's not much," he said at last. He'd always been grey but now he was beginning to go bald. It was her greatest fear – that she would lose her luxuriant hair – but it was all right for men to epilate (as John had called it). She had it added to the long list of life's unfairnesses against women that they sometimes did so too. "Thousands of people use taxis for hospital appointments."

Frazier, because he was an insubordinate fat bloke, said with a noticeable degree of sarcasm, "But there aren't many taxi drivers who dump burned arms into waste bins in the park."

"Perhaps he didn't know what it was," responded Lambert.

"He must have done. It was quite obvious that it was a human arm, sir."

Having ignored Frazier's tone, Lambert rounded on her. "And what have you done to identify this taxi and the driver?"

Bayes interjected, "Unfortunately, we couldn't get a registration number from the witness."

"Not even a partial?"

"No. All she said was that it was a dark colour. Dark blue or black, she thought."

Beverley added, "Her description of the driver is fairly generic, too."

She thought she heard Lambert grind his teeth but decided that that was fanciful. He asked, "And the taxis that took Mervyn Bridgeman to and from his hospital appointment?"

"We've talked to the driver of the one that took him. It's a white VW people carrier. The driver's female."

"And the one that picked him up from the hospital?"

"We haven't located it. Enquiries at the hospital haven't helped, I'm afraid. So many people come and go, and so many taxis turn up there that no one we've spoken to has been able to help us."

Was that a growl? Surely not, Superintendent . . . Beverley kept her face straight. Lambert really was a case, but surely he wasn't so far gone as to actually grind his teeth and growl?

"Are we even sure that the arm belonged to a torso that we've found?" he asked sarcastically.

"There's a DNA match with one of the three torsos in Kinison's kitchen."

Lambert seemed to be thinking about this, but Beverley suspected that he was just thinking about the next weakness he could probe in order to bring her down. He asked, "Where are the post-mortem reports on those three? I haven't seen anything."

Everyone looked at her. She had to pick the words with care, "They haven't been done . . ."

He was glaring at her ferociously as he interrupted. "You what?" He didn't shout. He didn't need to. "They haven't been done?" If incredulity had weight, Lambert's four words would have dropped through reinforced concrete. "Why not?"

"Our pathologist . . ."

"Eisenmenger, yes . . ."

"He didn't turn up . . ."

Lambert jumped. "He *what*?"

"And I haven't been able to contact him since . . ." She kept her voice steady which she considered to be something of a triumph, albeit one she could never celebrate.

"For fuck's sake!"

Lambert was very red in the face. He jabbed a finger at Beverley. "To my office. Now."

She followed him out of the meeting room but not before she caught sight of Frazier's expression, one of pure schadenfreude.

*

"I knew it was a mistake."

"Eisenmenger's the best."

Lambert looked directly into her face. "The best at what, Wharton?" There was almost a leer in the question.

"The best at forensic pathology, sir." She saw no point in rising to his bait.

"But you and he had a relationship, didn't you? For all I know, you might still be having one."

"I wanted John Eisenmenger because he's a brilliant pathologist."

"He's flaky." She couldn't in truth argue with Lambert about that. *Still, it's not like him just to disappear.*

"He was involved in a hit and run."

"Are you using that as an excuse for him? Is that the problem?"

"No. I talked to him after the incident. He was going to perform the autopsies for us."

"He didn't turn up."

"I have information that makes me think that he might be in danger."

"Amaze me, Chief Inspector."

"He took a taxi from the hospital."

There was a pause. "And?" Lambert's voice was dangerous.

"I think he may have been kidnapped. I think he may be in the hands of our killer . . . sir."

"Because he got a taxi home from the hospital."

"Yes, sir."

"And that's it?"

"Yes, sir."

Lambert squinted at her, then shook his head. "Bollocks."

"We don't know that for certain. All we know is that he appears to have vanished."

"Whatever's happened to him, Wharton, we need the post-mortems done."

"Yes, sir."

He thought for a moment. "Get Sydenham."

"Charles Sydenham?"

"You heard."

"But . . ."

"But what?"

"He's crap."

The wasp evidently chose that moment to sting him somewhere in his fundament. He growled, "If Eisenmenger can't be arsed to turn up when he's wanted, then we need a replacement. We need autopsies to be done on those three torsos, and we need them done as soon as possible."

She couldn't argue with the truth of that. She stood, assuming that the encounter was over, but he then asked, "Did you get a psychological profile, as I told you to?"

"Yes, sir." She had, although it was one of the very many reports she hadn't read. She hadn't even read the summary.

"And?"

"It didn't tell us anything we didn't already know."

"I want to see it."

He sounded to her ears petulant. "I'll make sure it's with you within the hour, sir."

Chapter Thirty-Two

Where are you, John?

She had rung the doorbell of Eisenmenger's small house four times – the last time leaning on it and practically pushing the button into the brickwork, as if *that* would make any difference – and been completely unsuccessful. She had thought that perhaps he might have gone to ground in there, had suffered some sort of total mental breakdown, but she doubted that now. She had eschewed shouting through the letterbox, though. Perhaps she should . . .

The door next along opened. A man in a pink cravat, white dress shirt, dark chinos and crimson smoking jacket came out. He was thin, about seventy years old and moustached. His thin fingers, stained yellow with nicotine on the right, fluttered. "He's not there."

"No."

"Hasn't been there for a day or two. I said to Jeremy, 'He's gone off again.'"

"So it would seem."

"He usually tells us, but not this time."

"Perhaps it was a sudden decision." She had things to do. She didn't want to stay to chat with this man. The man eyed her up and down. "You came here a couple of days ago, didn't you?"

She was surprised and annoyed, although she didn't show it. "That's right."

"You stayed the night. Jeremy and I saw you leave."

Neighbours. Sometimes she loved 'em. Oftentimes she hated 'em.

"That's right."

He nodded. "Are you close to him?"

No false hesitations, no attempts to pretend to sensitivity. She could grow to like this man. "Yes."

"Beverley, am I right?" She was surprised but nodded. "Wait here."

He disappeared back into his house. She waited, although she thought that she really ought to be heading back to the station. Lambert wouldn't be long in missing her and the last thing she needed was that old prick on her case about wasting time . . . What had the old man gone for, anyway? And who was he, other than a nosy neighbour? He lived with Jeremy, but she didn't yet know his name. Did that matter?

He returned, holding up keys. "If you're worried about him, I can let you in."

"I don't know . . ." He was already heading for Eisenmenger's front door.

He turned. "He said that if you came calling and we saw you, we were to let you in."

"He did? When?"

"Oh, ages ago."

When they had been a couple . . . Still . . .

He nodded, stared at her briefly, smiled, then turned back to the door. It was double-locked but they were soon inside. He looked around, she thought, hungrily. "He's definitely not here," he said after peering into the kitchen and craning his neck upstairs, and calling out.

"No, he's not, is he?" This was to herself. She was distinctly worried, although the precise reasons for this were far from distinct to her. She wandered into the kitchen. The notebook he had tried to get her to read was still there, exactly where she had left it. She picked it up.

Surely not . . .

Chapter Thirty-Three

"Johnny's gone AWOL, then."

Charles Sydenham couldn't help sounding nasty, she knew. She had often speculated how deep it went with Sydenham, and whether there was a mewling, puking, self-doubting nerd just below the surface that he presented to the world. As a pathologist, it was her opinion that Eisenmenger's farts were of more value than Sydenham's words, and she was sure it wasn't just because she had slept with Eisenmenger. Did Charles Sydenham allow himself to have half an inkling of that truth? She doubted it.

She looked across at Bayes, who hadn't encountered the tall, patrician pathologist before, wondering if he could see through him. Perhaps, perhaps not; maybe it would just take time, or maybe she would have to guide him to the Truth. He certainly seemed to be taken in at present, appearing to hang on Sydenham's words as if they glittered with golden truth.

"We don't know what's happened to him," she replied warily before Bayes could reply.

Sydenham had on a green wrap-around gown and plastic apron over his day clothes. He had no mask or cap. *Proper old school*, she thought. He snorted. "He never could keep a clear separation between work and his personal life." He looked meaningfully at Beverley so that she had to look away to stop blushing.

Bayes asked, "What's that got to do with anything?"

Sydenham switched his attention to the sergeant. "He took things to heart, did Johnny."

"You speak as if he's dead."

Sydenham guffawed. "He's buggered off somewhere, I expect. Things got too much for him, no doubt. He's probably sobbing to himself in a darkened room."

Beverley asked icily, "Be that as it may, Charles. What findings have you got for us?"

He was on his third and last torso. "I don't know what you expect, given that these are effectively only half-bodies."

"Any idea of cause of death?"

He didn't even reply verbally to that, contenting himself with a look of disdain and a curt shake of his head.

"What about torture?" asked Bayes. "Doctor Eisenmenger reckoned that they might be acid splashes." He indicated irregular ulcers on the fronts of two of the torsos.

Sydenham laughed nastily. "Nice theory; just what I expect from my esteemed colleague."

"You don't agree?"

"Never speculate with insufficient data, Sergeant. Know who said that?"

"I think you've just paraphrased Sherlock Holmes, haven't you?"

If Sydenham was taken aback at this display of literary knowledge, he didn't show it, of course. "Exactly."

"A fictional detective," pointed out Beverley.

Sydenham looked at her with open contempt. "I wouldn't be so gung-ho as to suggest *what* caused them at this stage. They *could* be burns – either acid or fire – but equally they could be natural."

"Natural?"

"Some skin diseases can cause open ulcers like that," responded Sydenham loftily. "Lymphoma and the like."

"On two of them?" she asked derisively. "You think they both had lymphoma? Is it that common?"

Sydenham didn't miss a beat. "I am not going to spec-ulate at present, Beverley." He smiled; or at least his lips lengthened and thinned, but it was much as an alligator had a wide smile that betokened no mirth whatsoever.

Bayes leaned over the low plastic wall that separated them from the dissection room proper. "Could any of them have been tramps?"

"Perhaps."

"Any distinguishing features?"

"None."

"Have you taken DNA samples?"

"Of course."

"Is there anything more you can say about them?"

"Not at the moment."

Beverley asked tiredly, "What about the arm, then? Can you give us anything useful about that?"

"Ah!" He turned and waved at White who was standing deferentially at the back of the dissection room. "Neil, bring on the arm."

He substitutes showmanship for acumen, she decided. She looked at Bayes and saw, with some relief, that he wasn't taken in.

Sydenham now had the arm. It was unwrapped and extensively burned. "As you can see, there's a tremendous amount of fire damage . . ."

"Too much to say anything useful? Is that what you're saying?" Bayes sounded irritated, Beverley thought. "Does it fit any of the torsos?"

Sydenham looked behind him. "I'd say it came from that one." He pointed at the torso that White had just finished sowing up.

"What else?"

Sydenham peered over his half-moon glasses at Bayes. "There are a couple of other things that might be of interest."

"What?"

Sydenham hefted the arm, spinning it slightly. Much of

the flesh of the arm itself had been burned off leaving only charred bone, except at the wrist; three fingers of the hand were also just bone, except for where the signet ring had been. There was no thumb and only the little finger had some remaining, albeit severely burned, flesh still attached.

"No fingerprints, I'm afraid, but I understand the signet ring has proved helpful . . ."

"What about the thumb?" asked Beverley.

"I'd say it was removed prior to the incineration, if that's what you mean."

"But before or after death?"

He looked up at her, a frown doing nothing for him. "Who can say?" She might have been about to reply but he continued quickly, "There are these marks here."

He pointed at the wrist.

"What are they?"

"Well . . ." His pause was long, unnecessary and exceedingly irritating to both police officers. ". . . It *could* be due to a shackle. It would have to have been a very tight shackle, of course."

With which he stripped off his gloves, and smiled, as if he had just solved the case for them.

Lambert was waiting for them when they returned to their office. He forget to say, "Hello," launching straight into, "Did you actually read this report?" He waved the forensic psychologist's profile at them.

"Of course." She had no difficulty lying, especially to the likes of Lambert. Bayes nodded.

"Then you know what the profiler concluded?"

She opened her mouth, still searching for a lie that would satisfy him. Bayes, though, said, "He thought it highly likely that there were two of them." Bayes turned to her. "Isn't that what you told me, sir?"

She smiled. "That's right, Sergeant." And she was, she thought, good too as she said it, hiding her confusion quickly and well. Lambert was clearly still suspicious but looking from Bayes to her and back again, now uncertain. Bayes added, "He thought they were likely to be very close, didn't he?"

She nodded. Lambert's eyes narrowed. "How is this influencing your investigation?"

She knew that she had to take control, that Lambert would expect no less. "It's not."

He looked almost comically taken aback. "What?"

"It's bollocks, Superintendent."

"What?" he repeated, only in a higher register. She quite enjoyed hearing it. In fact, she was quite enjoying the whole experience now.

"Two perpetrators? Two?" she asked. "Is he seriously suggesting that two of them are at work here? That would be a first . . ."

"What about the Wests?" This from Bayes.

She turned around at once, her face thunderous. She said tightly, "They were the exception that proved the rule."

She turned back as Lambert said, "Nevertheless, Chief Inspector, I don't want you to ignore this, understand?"

"Until we identify a suspect, I don't see how it can help, sir."

She judged that it had just the right amount of impertinence in her tone that he wouldn't react, not while her words were apparently designed to assuage him. He threw the report down on her desk. "Well, bloody well find a suspect, Wharton. The clock's ticking, don't forget."

"I'm well aware of that, sir."

He went to the door. "You've just been at the autopsies of the latest victims, is that right?"

"Yes."

"Did Sydenham do them?"

"As you ordered."

"Learn anything useful?"

She shook her head, and kept her voice straight. "Nothing we can use at the moment."

"You're sure of that? You're not just saying that because it was Sydenham?"

"You'll have his report as soon as I do, sir. You'll be able to see for yourself."

He nodded curtly.

Chapter Thirty-Four

Eisenmenger came to in a solid wooden chair, in agony. He felt as if he had been kicked in the side of the chest and the pain that he knew would come when he tried to breathe in came at him with redoubled intensity. His right knee, now divested of any support and bent at a right ankle, throbbed. His head ached abominably, too. And he was cold. He was cold because he was completely naked. He shivered. He looked around, making his head hurt terribly. He was shackled at the wrists and the ankles, and he could feel that they were so tight they were already rubbing his skin.

He could guess in general where he was, although the specifics eluded him. He was very, very scared indeed. He didn't want to end up without limbs or head, having been tortured, but he knew instinctively that here was where it had happened to at least ten others.

The fear added to his pain. The pain added to his fear. Despite it all, he tried to look around with an eye that was objective, that only saw the things that were around him, not their connotations. It was impossible, though.

He was in the middle of a room that was painted red, even the floor. At first, he couldn't locate a window of any type; perhaps there was one behind him, he wondered but did so groggily, and thus he couldn't see it; if there was one, no light came through it as far as he could see. Directly opposite him was a full-length mirror that reflected him. He tried not to look at himself, but couldn't resist it, despite the shudders that seeing himself naked brought on; behind him. The reflection went in and out of focus, but above and behind him he saw wooden board across a window of some sort. To the left of the mirror there was a dark brown door, with three panels that were heavily padded; even *that* looked sinister in the light from a single bare bulb that hung from the centre of the ceiling. It was an energy-saving bulb, he saw. He looked down to the floor. It, too, was red, but there were vague stains on it. He didn't want to think what those might be.

Every breath hurt . . .

He felt himself beginning to panic and clamped down hard on it. It would do no good for him. He tried to assume a dispassionate, analytical frame of mind, to work out what had happened him and, perhaps more intriguingly, why.

Was it related to the hit and run of the day before, but was it therefore chance that he now found himself here?

Was it all related in some way to the hospital? In which case, was there conceivably a connection with Claire Woodforde's suspicions? If so, how? There was a world of difference between the subtlety that a hospital killer must have, and the kind of person who had been torturing and dismembering men. And the men . . . Why him? He was a single man, true, but surely he didn't fit with the profiles of the other victims? Mind you, they hadn't all been vagrants, or ex-convicts, and they hadn't been able to identify very many of them . . .

His head throbbed . . .

How had he come to the notice of the killer, then?

How had he come to be here? He remembered getting into the taxi, the driver turning towards him, and then saying something . . . He remembered the car moving away from the hospital, and driver talking aimlessly as taxi drivers do . . . He remembered the journey to his house with some difficulty; why should that be? He just about recalled arriving outside his house, but . . .

His door had been locked so that he couldn't get out of the car. He had looked across at the driver, but he was already outside of the car. It was at this point that he remembered becoming bewildered. The driver had looked around, and then he had turned, bent down and looked directly at Eisenmenger. He had been smiling . . .

And with that, Eisenmenger had known no more.

What had it been? Gas, he guessed.

What should he do now? Shout? Wouldn't his predecessors have tried that? Try to move the chair? He looked down; it was bolted down. He knew already that he wouldn't be able to get out of the shackles on his wrists and ankles.

There came a sudden noise from the other side of the brown door. Bolts being drawn back. He tensed himself, saw a frightened man in the mirror.

Chapter Thirty-Five

"You'll never believe this . . ."

"Try me." She wasn't in the mood for this shit. Eisenmenger's notes lay on her desk in front of her, and she didn't think much of the theories therein.

Hypotheses, not "theories" . . .

Where the fuck had that come from? She looked at Bayes but, of course, he wouldn't – couldn't – have said that kind of thing, which was the kind of thing that . . .

. . . Only John would say . . .

Bayes said, "A head's turned up."

Which caught her attention as very few sentences could have done.

"Where?"

Frazier came into the office, eating a twelve-inch sub.

"On a roof."

Even as he tucked into his sandwich, Frazier looked interested.

She asked, "A roof? Where?"

Frazier asked, "What's going on?"

"In the city centre."

She stood up, Eisenmenger and his hypotheses forgotten. "What are we waiting for?"

They left, Frazier and his sandwich trailing behind them, a puzzled look on his face.

*

The view of the cathedral was spectacular, even in those circumstances, with the rain beating down, the wind blowing across the roofing felt and a rotten head producing a downwind stench that would have made a stone statue puke. If she turned around, she could see the river, the surface of the water choppy. It was cold, too; cold enough to make her shiver. She hoped that no one was watching her; *never show weakness*. This mantra had become part of her internal rhythm and rhyme from day one in the service. *Never.*

She asked Bayes, "How the hell did anyone find out it was up here?"

Frazier pointed at the six-storey building over the road. "A woman on the fifth floor spotted it. She was in a meeting about . . ." He looked down at his notebook. ". . . Sexually transmitted diseases, or something . . ." He looked up at her, then quickly down again. "She swears it wasn't here yesterday."

There had been a part of her that had been worried that it would be Eisenmenger's head; she hadn't shown her relief when she had arrived and discovered a stranger's decaying head.

"How would you say it got up here?" As she spoke, the wind blew hard and cold and she fought to keep her voice steady. She succeeded, too.

He was peering over the edge of the roof. "It could have been thrown up here. It's only one storey, after all."

"That's what I thought."

"Hell, it might have been done it from a moving car."

"If there were two of them," she pointed out. "And be careful. I don't want to lose you."

His head snapped round to look at her, surprised by her words. He stepped back from the edge.

Sydenham arrived, climbing awkwardly up the ladder. He looked old, she thought, in his anorak. "Is it safe?" were his first words through the patter of the falling rain, called as he clung to the top of the ladder, before setting a single, careful foot on the roof. His hood was up.

"Don't worry. You can walk on it."

"What?"

"You can walk on it, Charles," she called more loudly. "But some of the ducts are hot."

Galvanised steel ducts – presumably part of the heating system of the building – ran across the roof. Sydenham hesitated before stepping onto the dark green of the roofing felt, then just stood there for a moment as if testing his weight on the surface. "Come on, Charles," she called. "Don't you believe me? We're here and we haven't fallen through, have we?"

He didn't reply directly but he did step forward away from the ladder. "A head, I understand," he shouted. "I can smell it, but I can't see it."

The rain had splashed his glasses and his trousers were wet from the knees to the unfashionable turn-ups; his red anorak had darkened as the water soaked in. He looked, she decided, pathetic. Bayes approached him. "It's over there, Doctor."

In truth, it shouldn't have been hard to spot, she thought, since it was surrounded by four crime scene officers, even if he couldn't see it directly. Sydenham advanced soggily towards them, calling, "Have you lot finished poncing around? Let me through, then."

They looked up at him, but most of them knew him well and they parted as he strode amongst them. One of them tried to point out that he was contaminating the scene, but he ignored her. He bent down over the head that lay on its side. Beverley walked over and stood just behind him as the crime scene officers stood to one side in a disgruntled huddle. Without looking up at her, he said, "I don't need to say much, do I, Beverley? Obviously, this head belongs to one of your torsos, and obviously we now have a cause of death."

"He was hit with something."

Sydenham had put on some white plastic gloves that he had taken from his pocket. He reached out and lifted the head by the lank black hair. It was very decayed; the skin was green and bloated, the eyes sunken and dried. Something unpleasant dripped out of it and splattered on the roofing felt. It was dark with green-grey spots.

"What's that?" asked Frazier who was now standing beside Beverley.

"A mix of blood and brain matter, I'd say." Sydenham looked over his shoulder at Frazier, who looked slightly distressed at this news.

The expression on the face was one of pain, she now saw; she could also see why. There were several circular depressions on top of it.

"How many of those are there?" asked Beverley.

He looked around the head while holding it up, deciding at last, "Five." Then he added, "Although they're of different depths."

"What do you think made them?"

He looked up at her. "What do *you* think made them?"

"A hammer?"

He smiled broadly. "Exactly my thought."

She felt sick and turned away. Bayes asked, "Are you all right?" There was genuine concern in his voice which he kept low.

She nodded, took a deep breath of cold air, and said,

"Get a statement from the woman who alerted us, and then find out all you can about this building."

She began to walk away.

"Where are you going?" he called after her.

"Back to the station." She suddenly felt very tired and, accountably, worried.

Chapter Thirty-Six

Eisenmenger immediately recognised the man who came into the room.

The taxi driver. He was dressed in the same clothes as he'd been in when driving the taxi. Expensive-looking jeans, a very neatly ironed shirt, brown shoes that were highly polished and highly pointed. He had a small moustache, too. Eisenmenger had never liked moustaches. Go the whole beardy hog, or go home, had always been his opinion.

"So, you're a pathologist."

"And you're a sadistic killer." He breathed too deeply; it hurt his side as if he had been stabbed. *Shit!*

"I've never had a pathologist in here before."

"No?" he asked breathlessly.

"No."

"Did you try to run me over?"

"It seemed like a good idea at the time."

"Did it? Why?"

He took a breath, thought about the answer to that. "You struck me as a handsome man."

"So you decided to kill me?"

"Each man kills the thing he loves . . ."

The man stood just inside the room. Eisenmenger noted that he had shut the door behind him quite carefully; were there other people in the house?

Oscar Wilde? Really? "What's your name?" he enquired, trying to keep his voice steady.

"You're John Eisenmenger."

"Are you afraid to tell me? Is that it?"

The taxi driver stepped further into the room. With a smile, he said, "A bit of housekeeping, Doctor . . ."

"What?" Eisenmenger was genuinely surprised. What did he mean?

"Before you ask, you're in a room that's been completely soundproofed." It gave Eisenmenger no pleasure to have his suggestion proved right. Not this one; not at this time. "Some of the others tried shouting, but to no effect other than giving themselves sore throats."

"Why do you do this?"

"I'm afraid I can't afford to give you toilet breaks." *What does that mean?* Eisenmenger genuinely didn't know. Before he could ask, the other said, "So you'll have to relieve yourself where you sit?"

"Even shit?"

The driver laughed. It was without mirth. "I doubt you'll be here that long."

Eisenmenger knew what *that* meant. He tried not to show the fear that was taking hold of him. "Where are we?" he asked. His reflection in the mirror suggested that he was unsuccessful.

"I'm not going to start hurting you yet, so you have a few hours."

"To do what?"

The taxi driver shrugged and smiled unpleasantly but said nothing. He began to walk around Eisenmenger. They both knew that the only thing Eisenmenger could do was worry. Eisenmenger asked, "Are you going to feed me?"

"No."

"At least tell me your name."

The taxi driver came close to his face. He looked down Eisenmenger's body. "Not bad, I suppose," he said. He looked back up. "Considering your age."

Eisenmenger couldn't stop himself glancing at the mirror for just a second. He had been well aware of the effects of the years upon his body. He knew that he had a paunch, that his muscles had gradually dissolved and weakened, that his skin had lost elasticity, that his bones had thinned. This apparent compliment scalded him. He knew that it was said by a man in the grip of psychosis, yet he couldn't at that moment – naked, hurting all over – divorce the words from his own feelings of inadequacy. He felt ashamed, no matter how hard he tried otherwise.

He tried hard, though. "Were the others better looking?" Which gave the taxi driver pause. "Some of them," he decided. Then, he giggled. It was a disturbing sound, hinting that somewhere deep inside him the control systems were breaking down. "At least I didn't have to wash you."

The vagrants.

He said, "Why do you do it?"

There was no response for a long time. He just looked at Eisenmenger appraisingly. Then, "For many reasons."

"Like what?"

He came right up to Eisenmenger, perhaps just staring into his face, possibly even breathing in the smell of his fear. Eisenmenger wanted to pull back but couldn't. As he just stood there in front of Eisenmenger, he closed his eyes; he could have been asleep. He said oneirically, "Partly because I like you . . ."

Of course.

"And partly because I like to hear you scream . . ."

Eisenmenger looked at him as he said this. He was smiling, of course.

Eisenmenger's voice was husky as he asked, "Why dismember them?"

At which the taxi driver opened his eyes, blinked as if he had been asleep, pulled away and shook his head sadly. "Now, now . . ."

He walked behind the chair, out of Eisenmenger's sight. There was a squeaking noise and he reappeared, pushing a wooden trolley. It would have been comical, had it not been carrying a large array of carpentry tools, knives, glass vials and a blowtorch. He left it directly in front of Eisenmenger. He spotted also a sharpened screwdriver, several razor blades and a packet of cigarettes. All of it was neatly arranged, though; the long instruments were parallel to one another, the glass vials stood in a straight line to one side, the razor blades sat in a line on green baize.

"Something for you to look at. To pass the time."

He looked at it, moved a glass vial just a millimetre to the left; Eisenmenger almost heard him sigh in satisfaction. Then he walked to the door, then turned. "I'll be back," he said in a guttural voice, a poor imitation of Arnold Schwarzenegger, and then winked.

Chapter Thirty-Seven

Frazier came into the office. "The prison connection was a bust."

"Nothing?"

"None of the other victims we've been able to identify ever spent time there."

It would have been too easy, she knew. Bayes came in, but he wasn't as dejected as Frazier.

"The head belonged to Owen Richardson."

"How do you know?"

"He had a record, so we had a photograph."

"A record for what?"

"He was a vagrant, last seen four months ago near Cirencester."

"Please tell me we've already found his torso, Bayes."

"His blood group was B positive; that matches one in

the shed. Same degree of decay. We'll know for sure when we get the DNA results back."

"Tell me all you know about Owen Richardson."

"As I said, he was down and out. Had a charge sheet that included the usual – you know, drunk and disorderly, theft etc., etc. . . ."

"Which torso was he?"

"Number four is the one with blood group match." They'd numbered them from the ground up.

She pulled up the post-mortem report on torso number four, speed-reading through it. Tortured with a thin blade and a cigarette; a healing stomach ulcer. Nothing else of use. She asked, "What have you got on the building where his head was found?"

Bayes said, "Like most of those buildings around the docks, it's unoccupied and up for sale. The present owners are . . ." He checked his screen. "Phalanger Ltd."

"What do they do?"

"Did – they've filed for bankruptcy."

"What *did* they do?"

"They were printers."

"Anything left inside the building? Did you check?"

"It's completely empty."

"Have forensics gone over it?"

He nodded. "Nothing."

"So, we can assume it was chosen at random?"

"I would say so. I would say it was thrown up there in the night."

"But why?" she asked. "Why distribute these things around the city? It's insane."

There was silence in the room until Frazier said tentatively, "Perhaps that's the answer."

"What do you mean?"

Frazier's expression suggested that he wished he hadn't said anything. He was slow in replying, "Maybe it's because the killer isn't thinking straight."

"Maybe he thinks it's all a big joke," suggested Bayes.

She said thoughtfully, ". . . Yes, there might be something in that . . . Maybe he's doing it to throw us off balance."

Bayes' voice was hesitant. "The profiler suggested something along those lines . . ."

Her stare was hostile.

"The profiler suggested as many things as he could cram in," she replied coldly. She had read the report purely for self-defence, not believing a word of it. "All this speculation is very interesting, but it doesn't get us any further forward in identifying the killer."

She returned to Eisenmenger's house that evening. She had retained the key and let herself in. She carried with her his notes. They wouldn't leave her alone, although she couldn't say why. Did what he had been doing at the hospital have something to do with his disappearance? Was it connected to the hit and run accident? No one had seen anything useful and, as it wasn't a fatal accident, it had quickly been relegated to the list of cases that would never be properly investigated.

But now you've disappeared . . .

She wandered around his house, memories stirring. She went into the bedroom. His bedroom . . . *their* bedroom once, and not so long ago. She went back down the narrow stairs and into the kitchen, checked in the fridge, finding, as she expected, several bottles of white wine. Good white wine, too. Of course. John Eisenmenger enjoyed the good life, especially when it came to drinking wine. She knew he wouldn't mind if she helped herself, and she accordingly poured herself a glass. This she took into the small front sitting room and sat down in an easy chair, his notes on the hospital deaths on her lap. She didn't know why she thought it was important, but she could feel significance in every word.

She opened it up at the first page for perhaps the seventh time, reading and drinking, not stopping until she came to the end. Then she put her head back and looked at the ceiling, trying to think.

His theory had been that all the cases identified by Claire Woodforde had passed through the Emergency Department . . . And that was it?

For God's sake, John. Was that it?

She knew enough about hospitals to know that patients either came in because they were required to come in for a procedure, or they came in as emergencies. Emergencies took priority, hence the shortage of beds for elective cases. She was sure that Eisenmenger had told her that emergencies had a worse prognosis, which made sense, but that led her to the question of how anyone could know that there had been an excess of deaths at the hospital amongst them . . .

"Shit, John," she sighed.

She returned to his notes.

Chapter Thirty-Eight

Eisenmenger shouted anyway, although a part of him knew that it was a useless act. It was shortly after this that he had pissed himself. He had held on for as long as he could but, having let go, he knew how stupid he'd been. There was no point to it. The whole point was that he *should* piss himself. It was part of the torture, part of the humiliation that the taxi driver wanted to inflict on his victims. At first it felt good to Eisenmenger – the pain in his bladder going gradually as he allowed the urine to flow – but it wasn't long before it felt uncomfortable on his legs. And then it felt cold, and then it felt as if it were burning him.

"Bastard," he whispered.

He was ravenous. Part of the torture, he knew. That knowledge didn't stop him being very hungry. He had tried to sleep but with little success. He didn't know whether it was day or night, although his body clock whispered to him that the night had died, as he would probably in short order. It would be painful, too. Probably intensely so. And there was nothing he could do to prevent the pain, because this was torture for the sake of sadism, not information. The more he screamed, the higher he screamed, the more he begged for mercy, the better.

He had tried not to chafe his wrists and ankles under the metal shackles, but couldn't help it. He had to move to relieve the pressure on his buttocks and the backs of his legs, and even this slight shift meant that, after God knew how many hours, he was rubbing his wrists and ankles raw under the tight metal shackles.

The door opened.

*

Beverley spent the night in John's bed, but with little sleep accrued. She rose, showered, dressed, then returned to his notes on the hospital deaths, a mug of unsweetened black coffee at her side. At eight, she phoned Bayes. He sounded tired, she thought.

"Work out the average age of the torsos."

"What?"

She repeated the command.

"You mean the time since death?"

"No," she said impatiently. "I mean the ages of the deceased."

"We've only got definite identification of three."

"But we've got estimates of age from the PM reports."

"May I ask why?"

"Because I want to know." She cut the connection. Then she phoned the infirmary switchboard. "Can you put me through to Doctor Claire Woodforde please?"

There was no answer. *Too early*, she thought, looking at her watch; it was twenty past eight. The hospital operator came back on the line. "It's too early," she said.

"She's an anaesthetist. Is that right?"

"Yes."

"Thanks."

By the time she got to the infirmary, it would be ten to nine. She would see Dr Woodforde in person.

*

"John Eisenmenger's gone missing."

Claire Woodforde was at once defensive. "What's that got to do with me?"

"Nothing directly."

"Then, I don't understand."

"But it might have something to do with what he was looking into here."

"I don't see how."

In truth, neither did Beverley, but she would never have admitted it. She said, "I've read his notes."

"And?"

"You gave him details of various patients that in your opinion had died when they shouldn't have."

"I know what I did, Inspector."

Beverley couldn't be bothered to correct her about the rank. It happened so fucking often . . .

"In his notes, John commented that all the patients were young for the diseases they had."

Claire Woodforde flopped back in her chair. Beverley didn't like her; she didn't like Beverley. It happened. Beverley didn't give a shit. Dr Woodforde said sarcastically, "That was part of the reason I thought they were worth investigating."

"He also observed that all of them came in through the Emergency Department."

"As do seventy per cent of our patients."

Help me here, Dr Woodforde. We're on the same side.

"But you thought there was something about them that was odd . . ."

"They shouldn't have died."

"Surely, you can't say that. People die unexpectedly all the time, especially in hospital . . ."

The anaesthetist sighed. It was a theatrical sigh, one that irritated Detective Chief Inspector Wharton. The anaesthetist explained, "Yes. It's a *statistical* aberration, Inspector."

"But you've been inferring *specific* cases from *statistics*, Doctor."

They stared at each other for a moment that both thought was a long time.

"If you don't believe me . . ."

But Beverley was merely testing the evidence and finding no answers. She was still making eye contact with the doctor as she said, "The average age of the cases that you picked out was fifty, is that correct?"

"Yes. What of it?"

Her phone rang. It was Bayes. "The average age of the victims was fifty. Of course, there's a lot of . . ."

She pressed the red button on her phone and cut him off.

Chapter Thirty-Nine

The taxi driver asked, "How are things with you?" He was bright and cheery.

"Fairly fucking awful. How else would you expect things to be?" Eisenmenger didn't open his eyes. His voice cracked through dehydration. He was simultaneously very cold and very sore.

The taxi driver walked around Eisenmenger, examining the chair and its occupant. From behind Eisenmenger, he said, "Nice day out there."

"Cunt."

He walked around the chair, still smiling. He went to the trolley, picked up first a hammer and then put it down in favour of a razor blade. He looked at this without saying anything. Eisenmenger had opened his eyes and was looking at the man who held the blade between his right thumb and forefinger. Then, still smiling, he strode towards Eisenmenger and slashed across his chest.

Eisenmenger arched as far as he could and screamed as blood coursed freely down his chest, abdomen and legs, pooling around and under and between them on the chair. Eisenmenger's scream became a prolonged cry, then a groan, before dying away. The mirror reflected a man in extreme pain, whose torso was tensed and jerking forward.

The taxi driver came close to his face as he panted; he was still smiling. He held the razor blade up very close to Eisenmenger's face. "Language, Timothy," he said. "Language."

He straightened up, looked down at Eisenmenger, whose torso was now covered with brightly crimson blood. He walked to the door. Eisenmenger called out, "Is that it?"

He turned. He was smiling hungrily. "For now."

He left the room. Eisenmenger heard bolts being drawn across.

*

Lambert believed not a word of it. "This is bollocks."

"Of course, it *could* be a coincidence, Superintendent." She kept her face straight, so that he couldn't see that she was thinking what a penis he was. "But in my experience, coincidences that happen in the course of an investigation . . ."

"Coincidences happen all the time, Chief Inspector. It's because we live in a random universe."

He looked very pleased with himself. In fact, he leaned

back in his chair and looked so self-satisfied that she wanted to punch him in the face. *Not for the first time* . . . "Sometimes coincidences aren't coincidences, sir. Sometimes, they're events that are connected . . ."

He rose and put his clenched fists on the desk. He wasn't a particularly imposing person, but he had everything going for him, what with the light from the window behind him, and the size of his desk, and her seated position. "You're obsessed," he growled. "Just because Eisenmenger thought that there was something going on at the hospital . . ."

She found that she had had enough. She stood up and went to the door without saying a word, but with a furious expression on her face and a lot of deep, dark thoughts in her head.

"Where are you going?"

"To my office . . . sir."

"Forget this . . . rubbish. Find the real madman, before your career – such as it is – goes down the toilet and is flushed away forever."

Back in her office, Bayes looked up as soon as she came in. "What did he say?"

The lie came easily. "He said go ahead. We need to look at every possibility."

"I still don't see how . . ."

"Serial killers are usually lower social groups, right?"

"Usually, yes . . ."

"I want you and Frazier to check all the staff at the

hospital, but begin with the cleaners, the porters and the ancillary staff."

"That's a lot of staff, sir."

"Start with any that have contact with the Emergency Department."

"That's still . . ."

"At the same time I want you to get a list of everyone who's registered with the City Council as a taxi driver. Cross-reference the two lists."

His mouth opened again and for a long time he might have been about to protest but when words came, he said only, "Yes, sir."

Chapter Forty

The next time the door opened, Eisenmenger was feeling close to delirium due to dehydration. He had had to empty his bladder again and he could not escape the stink of stale urine that arose from the chair and his legs, nor the discomfort that he felt on the backs of his legs. The cut across his chest had stopped bleeding but not hurting. He could see from the mirror's reflection that his entire front below it was covered in sticky, clotting blood that pulled at his skin and was driving him mad. No matter how hard he had tried, the skin at his wrists and ankles had been chafed away; another source of agony.

The taxi driver asked, "How's things?"

Eisenmenger tried to speak, but his voice wouldn't come.

"Thirsty?" the man asked, as if the idea had only just come to him, as if the whole concept of dehydration for Eisenmenger was a novel one to him, as if the others that had preceded Eisenmenger in that chair had experienced nothing of the sort. Eisenmenger nodded, his mouth open, his eyes half shut.

"Wait here."

He left the room. Even through his half-delirium, Eisenmenger saw that he didn't close and bolt the door; not that there was anything he could do with that datum. Eisenmenger heard footsteps going down wooden stairs. Another piece of useless knowledge. Returning steps a few minutes, that to Eisenmenger might have been seconds or hours, later, and then footsteps ascending the stairs and the taxi driver's return to the room, bearing a full plastic bottle. He shut the door behind him quietly.

"Some water for you."

He held it up in front of Eisenmenger who opened his mouth and tilted his head back. The taxi driver poured it out of the bottle, but not directly into his mouth. He poured it over Eisenmenger's face and shoulders, splashing it freely. Eisenmenger sucked at the water, tried to anticipate where it was going to fall, so often getting it wrong.

And then the bottle was empty, and the cut on Eisenmenger's chest as bleeding again and hurting because of his wild movements, and he had a wet face and torso, and moisture in his mouth. He licked around his mouth as far as his tongue would allow, while the taxi driver laughed.

*

Frazier's summons to Lambert's office didn't fill him with trepidation; he wasn't capable of what would be required for such an emotion; if the situation demanded it, Frazier tended to think only three minutes ahead, and only then with some effort. He didn't like expending effort. Accordingly, he ascended the stairs to Lambert's floor – the top floor and the lifts weren't working, otherwise Frazier would have used them – reaching it very out of breath and red-faced. He paused, but not for long. He walked along the relatively luxurious carpet of the corridor, still panting. He knocked on Lambert's door.

"Come."

He entered. Lambert was writing something. Every time Frazier had been in a superintendent's office, the superintendent had been writing something. He supposed it went with the job. It made him glad that he would never be a superintendent.

Lambert looked up. "You're out of breath."

"The fucking lifts don't work, do they?"

Lambert stared at the obese junior. Frazier didn't give a shit and eventually Lambert said only, "You should go to the gym more."

"Yes, sir." The tone was totally at odds with the words; they both knew that Frazier wasn't about to go anywhere near a place that existed only to make people fitter through physical exercise.

Lambert returned to his writing; Frazier continued to

stand in front of the desk. His patience was built into every adipocyte he possessed. He could stand there all day; it was of no concern to him. Standing there in that office held for him several positives, not least that he didn't have to do any useful work.

At last, Lambert put down his pen. "What's DCI Wharton doing?"

"You mean now? At this moment?"

"Yes."

Frazier had no qualms about telling Lambert anything he wanted to know. His immediate problem was that he didn't precisely know what Lambert was talking about. "She's following your orders."

"What does that mean? What's she doing?"

"She's ordered Bayes and me to go through lists of council-registered taxi drivers."

Lambert nodded. "Good."

"And she's ordered us to cross-reference that list with people working at the hospital, especially those who work in the A and E Department . . ."

Lambert's eyes widened. "She what?"

Frazier repeated what he had said; he saw the reaction and was pleased. Generally his career had brought him into contact with such as Superintendent Lambert when he was going to be bollocked. He could see that he was at that moment in a special place.

Lambert thought about what Frazier had said; if it were true, Wharton was deliberately disobeying him. If *that* were true, he had her . . . He said to Frazier, "Okay. Go back down and carry on as she's ordered."

"You're sure?" Frazier didn't understand.

"I'm positive."

"Oh. Okay." Frazier felt cheated. Perhaps he wasn't in a special place, after all.

"But don't mention this conversation. Understand, Frazier?"

Frazier understood and was glad again.

Chapter Forty-One

"Dunant," said Bayes apropos of nothing at all.

"What?" asked Beverley.

"There's a taxi driver registered with the council called Henry Dunant."

"What of it?"

"One of the porters at the infirmary is also called Dunant. Paul Dunant."

She felt something akin to an electric shock, but forced herself to be calm. "Find out all you can about Paul Dunant."

"I'm on it."

She turned to Frazier. "And you bend your considerable detective skills to finding out all you can about Henry Dunant."

He frowned but contented himself with a small nod. They worked away for two hours, much of which Bayes spent on the phone, before he stood and went to her desk. "What have you got?" she asked.

"Paul Dunant used to be a medical student at Imperial College, but dropped out. He resurfaced as a porter at the infirmary three years later."

"Why did he drop out of medical school?"

"According to the deputy academic dean, there was a question about his involvement in the disappearance of certain controlled drugs."

"Controlled drugs? You mean opiates?"

Bayes nodded.

"But they didn't prosecute?"

"They would have done, but for the interjection of a senior consultant in the Accident and Emergency Department, who pleaded for mercy, claiming that there was no real evidence against Dunant."

"Who was that?"

"Peter Sulston."

She thought at once that she knew the name, but Bayes was ahead of her. "He now works in the Emergency Department at the infirmary."

"How interesting," she cooed.

"And even more interesting is the fact that, according to the Human Resources directorate at the infirmary, Sulston acted as one of Paul Dunant's employment references."

She stared at him, thinking hard. "Why would he do that?" she wondered.

He shrugged. She said, "Find out Sulston's address."

He moved back to his desk. She turned her attention to Frazier. "What have you got for me?"

Frazier looked up, then cleared his throat; despite this, his voice still croaked as he began. "Henry Dunant is fifty-five years old. He's been a taxi driver for eighteen years. He's married with three daughters. Lives in the city centre near the rugby ground."

"Fifty-five?"

It didn't sound like the man who had deposited the arm in the waste bin . . .

Bayes put down the phone, looking both disbelieving and triumphant. "Sulston's address is the same as Paul Dunant's."

She slapped the top of her desk, then stood up. "Come on, Bayes. We're going to the infirmary."

"What about me?" asked Frazier.

She stopped on her way to the door. "You? You can stay here." She thought of something. "And you can tell Lambert when he comes sniffing around where we've gone, and why we've gone there."

Bayes followed her out of the door, but his eyes were on Frazier, a quizzical expression playing around his features.

"What was all that about?"

Beverley drove. "What was all what about?"

"About telling Frazier to tell Lambert where we've gone and why we've gone there."

"It doesn't matter to you."

They drove on in silence.

*

"Paul Dunant?"

She saw fear at once and she felt good. They were in a corridor, just outside the Emergency Department. He said, "Yes?"

She showed him her warrant card; over her shoulder, Bayes did likewise. "We'd like to have a chat."

"I'm working."

"So are we."

He looked as if he wanted to run; he looked so much that way that Bayes tensed, especially when Dunant glanced up and down the corridor. He stayed where he was, though. All of the fight seemed to escape him as he breathed out. She asked, "Is there anywhere we can chat, Paul?"

First names are good. They reduce the tension, make things that aren't in any way equal appear fair and friendly.

He looked around, then shrugged. "Dunno. Outside?"

"Why not?" She smiled. She smiled well, she knew.

He had a walkie-talkie that he unclipped from his belt. "It's Paul. Ten-minute break."

The reply came replete with distortion and crackling, but still clear enough. "Don't smoke more than one, Paul."

They followed him out through the main entrance, past the shops and the coffee bar, never letting him get too far ahead. Outside, under the canopy and away from others' ears, he stopped and turned. "What's this about?"

"Your name is Dunant."

"So?"

"Are you a relative of Henry Dunant, the taxi driver?"

"He's my uncle." He produced a packet of cigarettes that he didn't offer around. From this he took a cigarette; he put it to his lips and lit it. The smoke was whipped away by the wind that took pleasure in blowing wickedly through the space under the canopy.

"Are you close?"

"I haven't seen him in years."

She looked at Bayes. He didn't understand, couldn't see that this wasn't going quite according to plan. *He's probably lying.* She took comfort from the thought; she was used to liars, they formed a familiar blanket for her. She said, "Where do you live, Mr Dunant?"

"Why?"

"Why not tell me?"

But he was reluctant and only after a long silence in which his cigarette pined away a bit between two fingers did he admit, "Leckhampton."

"Alone?"

He looked at her with fear and loathing in his eyes, she thought. *He's afraid that I already know, but he can't be sure . . .* He said, "I've got a partner."

"Male or female?"

Dunant looked at his watch. To their side, a family was congregated around the pay machine for the car park; they were cursing the charges. He said, "I haven't got long . . ."

"We appreciate that."

"So why are you asking about my private life?"

"Why don't you tell us?"

"What the fuck has it got to do with anything?"

"Do you live with a male or female?"

He lowered his gaze, took a drag and said to his shoes, "Male."

"By the name of Peter Sulston?"

He looked up, closed his eyes, and whispered, "Yes." He drew a lot of atmosphere through his cigarette; the tip burned brightly.

Chapter Forty-Two

"Does the name John Eisenmenger mean anything to you, Paul?"

Perhaps he really did think hard about this question; perhaps he was just a good actor. Beverley couldn't tell. They sat in Sulston's office, Beverley behind the desk, Dunant and Bayes at either end. Sulston was absent, but due into the department in short order, according to his disgruntled secretary who hadn't liked them intruding; no, not at all. Even the authority of the warrant cards hadn't done much for her gruntlement but, hey-ho, Beverley didn't give a finger-flicking fuck about that.

"I don't think so. Why? Should it?"

"He was brought into casualty a couple of days ago. A victim of a hit and run."

"Oh, him."

"You remember him?"

"Not the name. I remember a hit and run." He looked from Beverley to Bayes and back again. When neither said anything, he explained, "Most of the time, I don't get given the patients' names. I wasn't given his."

"But you met him?"

The corners of his mouth turned down as he nodded. "I took him to X-ray, I think . . ."

"And that's it?"

Frowning now. He said after a short pause, "I saw him the next day. He'd been discharged, but was still in a fairly bad way, limping and in obvious pain."

"You saw him?"

Dunant was relaxing more and more as the conversation went on, Beverley noticed. She wondered why. He said, "It's happening more and more."

"What is?"

"Discharging people when they're in no fit state . . ." He looked up and perhaps he saw something in their eyes, for he went on at once, "I got him a wheelchair. Took him to the coffee shop. He said something about a lift home from someone, but getting the bum's rush . . ."

"You left him at the coffee shop?"

"Yep."

"Nothing more?"

"Well, I gave him a tip for a taxi."

"A tip?"

"Yeah. You know, a card."

"Whose taxi firm do you recommend?"

He couldn't believe the stupidity of the question. "My uncle's."

Beverley could scent something. She didn't know what it was, though.

"Tell me about your uncle."

"I told you. I haven't seen him for ages."

"Years, you said. How many?"

"Two, maybe."

"Yet you're still handing out his cards?"

"I told him I would. I saw no reason to stop."

"Tell me about him."

But he didn't respond. He looked almost as if he had left the room.

She repeated, "Tell me about your uncle, Paul."

"What's all this about?"

"We think he might be involved in something."

"What?"

"Murder."

His pause was born of incredulity. "Murder? Uncle Henry? You're joking . . ."

"Why? Why am I joking?"

"He's kind . . . A gentler man you couldn't hope to meet."

She felt rather than saw Bayes pull back slightly, as if these words absolved Henry Dunant. She said doggedly, "I'm not hearing anything that reassures me, Paul. Nor am I hearing anything that makes me any less inclined to worry about you."

"Me?"

She nodded. "You."

"You're saying I'm a murderer? Who? Who have I killed?" He was comically belligerent, she thought.

"Too many people are dying in this hospital, Paul."

"So?"

"So you're in and out of the Emergency Department all the time."

"Do you know how difficult it is to get hold of controlled drugs? The clue's in the name."

Sarcasm's not a clever thing to roll out when in your situation, Paul . . .

In the corner of her eye, she saw Bayes look up abruptly. *You spotted it, too, then . . .*

To Paul Dunant, she pointed out quietly, "I never mentioned anything about controlled drugs." Which gave him pause; his gaze jerked between his interrogators and his fingers twitched. She knew that it was important not to let him think now. She said, "But you have a history, don't you, Paul?"

"I don't know what you mean."

"You were a medical student, once, weren't you?"

He flopped back in his chair. "Oh, that."

"Yes, that. Some little trouble about 'controlled drugs', wasn't it?"

"Nothing was proved."

"Only thanks to the intervention of a senior consultant." She judged the pause. "What was his name, now?"

"You know." He spoke grudgingly, almost sulkily. She mused how quickly he reverted to the mores of a child. How old was he? Thirty?

"Peter Sulston," she said in whisper, leaning towards him.

There was silence.

She went on, "Who works here now. Who is your partner. Who daily prescribes controlled drugs."

More silence.

It didn't bother her; she had things to say. "How does it work? I can think of one way; he gives a little less than is prescribed, and gives the rest to you. Over time, that might build into a considerable quantity, mightn't it?"

"I don't know what you're talking about."

The sound of raised voices intruded. The door opened violently and banged against a filing cabinet. A man entered. An angry man, Beverley observed, and deduced that he was Peter Sulston. His eyes looked around the room, but lingered on Dunant. The sight only increased his anger. "What the bloody hell is the meaning of this?" he demanded.

"Doctor Sulston?" she asked. She smiled. "Sorry to intrude, but we wanted privacy and your office was empty."

"What's going on?" he demanded, as if in a soap opera.

"We were talking to Paul, your partner, about various matters."

His look lingered on Dunant, she saw, before flicking first to Bayes and then to her. "What . . . matters?"

"About his uncle, Henry Dunant."

Sulston visibly relaxed. "The taxi driver?"

"That's the one." She waved at him. "Please, sit down."

There was one unoccupied chair; that he pulled it up to the desk and sat in it without argument pleased her enormously. She asked him, "Have you ever met Henry Dunant?"

"I don't think I have." He looked at Paul Dunant. "I haven't, have I?"

Dunant shook his head.

Beverley was minded to believe them. "Tell me what you know about him, then."

"Only that he owns a taxi firm . . ."

Before she could speak again, Bayes looked up at him. "A taxi firm?"

She was thinking that she would excoriate Bayes for intruding, but at that moment she knew better than to make this about the interrogators rather than the interrogated. She remained silent.

Sulston nodded. "Yes. That's what I understood."

He looked at his partner. "A firm, right?"

Dunant nodded. His eyes were wary as they stared at Bayes.

"How many cars?"

Beverley at last saw what Bayes had spotted. She would delay the excoriation.

Dunant replied, "At one time, he had four."

"And four drivers?"

"Three."

"Now?"

"Following the economic downturn, he had to downsize. It nearly killed him."

"How many drivers does he employ now?"

"It's just him and one other."

"What's the other's name?"

He shook his head. "Don't know."

Chapter Forty-Three

"The superintendent wants to see you."

Beverley's stare at Frazier analysed him, picked him apart, dissected him; in reality, he remained distressingly, repulsively whole, though. "Does he?"

"He sounded a bit pissed off."

"Did he?" She wasn't going to let Frazier press her buttons. She said to Bayes, "Get onto Henry Dunant. We need to talk to him."

"Where?"

"If he's at home, we'll go there. If he's out in his taxi, get him in here."

*

Someone had once decided that "White With a Hint of Apple" would be a good colour to paint the interrogation rooms. They hadn't had the foresight to see that the colour would fade to a shade of cream that Beverley could only describe as "dingy", but she couldn't blame them. Foresight was such a fickle thing, alighting on a single person for perhaps a moment, no more; interior designers – even the best – possessed it for no longer than anyone else. The smell didn't help either. Beverley had never *seen* anyone relieve themselves in that room, but a great many people had passed through over the years, and it was entirely possible that one or two of them had emptied their bladders, just as it was also likely that many of them had stunk to high heaven anyway. However it had got there, the stench lingered.

Henry Dunant had been out in his taxi. He explained in a high-pitched, anxious voice, "My wife, Fi, lets me know when a potential fare phones. I don't ply for trade on the streets . . ."

She heard only someone who was protesting too much as she sat opposite him.

"No?" She couldn't help herself, even though it was entirely irrelevant.

"Oh, dear, no. Never."

Which, she suspected, even Bayes could hear was a lie. She said, "Your company . . ."

"Dunant cars, yes."

He was at least five stone overweight, she judged. The consequence of sitting in a car for years, the only exercise pushing on pedals and pulling on a power-assisted steering wheel, the diet containing a large proportion of bacon sarnies and the occasional BLT for a few of his "five a day".

"What cars do you own?"

"Well, mine, of course . . ." He was sweating, and the flesh of his neck spilled over his collar; she wondered how he could stand having it done up, but done up it was, with a bright red tie. Political affiliation, she wondered?

"Which is what colour?"

"Silver. I think the manufacturers – Mercedes – call it 'Inca Silver'. Stupid name, but that's the kind of name that big companies think is clever . . ."

"A Merc?" she interrupted.

"Yes, a Merc . . ."

"You employ one other driver, don't you?"

"Yes. Frank. I used to employ more but, you know . . ."

He made a face that intimated to them that everyone knew what he was talking about. Bayes glanced up from his notebook, then down again. It was an informal interview and the tape machines weren't running, nor had Henry Dunant been cautioned. Bayes, though, was taking notes.

"Frank? What's his second name?"

"Aston."

"What does he drive?"

"What's all this about? He hasn't done something wrong, has he? Or me? Have I done something?"

"It's very kind of you to come in, Mr Dunant," she said soothingly. "It's just that we want to exclude Frank from our enquiries." She didn't, though. It was a lie. She desperately wanted Frank Aston to be the killer, because that would mean so many good things to her. "What kind of car does Frank drive?"

Dunant liked the idea of helping the police with their enquiries, she could see. Having been reassured, his answers came eagerly. "A Mercedes as well. I've always gone for Mercedes cars. Touch of class, I think. Don't you agree?"

Whether she agreed or not wasn't the point. She asked, "What colour?"

"That one's Midnight Blue . . ."

She exchanged a glance with Bayes.

"Describe Frank to me."

Which, as she had come to expect, proved inexplicably difficult for him. "Well . . . I don't know . . ."

"Tall or short?"

"Medium, I'd say."

"Fat or thin?"

"In between."

"Dark or fair?"

"Oh, fair. Definitely fair."

"Any distinguishing features?"

"How do you mean?"

"Scars, birth marks, that kind of thing."

"Not that I can think of."

"How old is he?"

"Twenty-nine."

"What kind of person is Frank?"

Henry Dunant suddenly became wary. "Why? He hasn't

done anything, has he? I know what people think about cab drivers . . ."

"Just tell me about Frank."

"A nice lad. I was impressed. I interviewed him, you know, with my wife. I don't want the company's reputation besmirched, so we've always taken on drivers only after careful consideration with the best references. We've always had a good reputation for cheapness, efficiency, courtesy and reliability. Always . . ."

Chapter Forty-Four

The taxi driver had changed his clothes, but was equally dapper. A tweed waistcoat over a pale lilac shirt that was open at the neck; black brogues and pinstripe trousers. He was sitting in front of Eisenmenger smoking a cigarette that he had ostentatiously lit from the blowtorch. Eisenmenger couldn't keep his eyes off the glowing tip, kept thinking, *Anywhere between four and nine hundred degrees Celsius . . .*

Wreathed in smoke, the driver said, "I felt something about you as soon as I saw you, but I wasn't sure for a long time what it was. But I researched you and I discovered that you have a certain . . . *knack*. Is that the word?"

"You surely don't expect me to argue, do you?" Eisenmenger could hear a lot of things in his own words, not least the fear that had grown monstrous as the hours had stretched past and he had had nothing to do but worry and look at himself in the mirror opposite.

The taxi driver looked surprised. "No, of course not." He laughed; a private joke. "Yes . . . A *knack*." He was pleased with the bon mot. "A knack for seeing your way through to the truth of situations, such as we have here."

Eisenmenger said nothing.

"Imagine my delight to have discovered that you are a bit of a loner. No wife, no girlfriend . . ." He breathed in the smoke as if it were a necessary component of the air that he breathed.

Perhaps he's finding the smell of ammonia too much to bear. He should try sitting in the fucking stuff.

"Thanks for reminding me."

He put the cigarette to his lips, pulled on it as he held it between forefinger and middle finger, then pointed at Eisenmenger as he breathed out smoke. "I didn't want you here, but I was persuaded otherwise." Eisenmenger's mind registered something, but the pain and the degradation he had to contend with made his mind slow. The young man looked at Eisenmenger quizzically, as if he couldn't believe even now the contrariness of humankind of which he was one. "But I now agree that you are too dangerous. You have to die."

"Because someone else says so?"

"Because I've decided it so."

"I'm just a pathologist . . ."

"But you're not, are you? You're a maverick. It's just lucky for us that you're a maverick in your social life . . ."

Eisenmenger licked his lips, finding no moisture. "Us?"

Eisenmenger was aware that he was goading this dangerous man, but he couldn't allow himself to despair. It was a question of mental survival.

The driver looked at him. "You know, I can't decide if it was good luck or bad luck that allowed you to fall into our hands."

"Our?"

The driver laughed. "*Our*, Doctor."

"So there are two of you?" Every question hurt; sometimes his head, sometimes his chest.

"Yes, Doctor." He sighed. "There are two of us. We are a pair, a couple, a twosome. Does that knowledge satisfy you?"

"Who's the other?"

No direct response. "Taking you was always going to be a risk, but we had no choice." His voice was sad.

"No choice?"

He thought about his next words as he sucked on the cigarette so that its tip glowed brightly. Eisenmenger watched it as it did so. The taxi driver looked at the tip and then at Eisenmenger. He stood up. He was smiling.

"What are you thinking?" Eisenmenger tried to keep the panic out of his voice as the taxi driver walked around the back of the chair, the cigarette still burning, now held upright.

"All sorts of things . . ." His voice, coming from directly behind Eisenmenger and distressingly close, was dreamy. In the mirror, Eisenmenger saw the taxi driver standing behind him, saw curling smoke coming from somewhere that wasn't visible to him . . .

And then there was agony in the back of Eisenmenger's neck and a smell of burning flesh and Eisenmenger screamed. In his ear, through the screams, he heard the taxi driver say softly, "And they're all so *fantastically* exciting."

Chapter Forty-Five

"He's had a terrible life, you see. And yet, despite it all, he's always so well turned out. That impressed Mrs Dunant and me, that did."

"In what way has his life been terrible, Mr Dunant?"

Henry Dunant was shaking his head, his adipose features twisted into an expression of sorrow and sympathy. It gave him a look that hinted at a gargoyle trying to be nice. Bayes had left the room as soon as Dunant had given them a name to check up on it. Dunant said, "Orphaned at three. Brought up by foster carers and then adopted into a family where he was bullied by two older brothers. He ran away when he was fourteen."

She didn't believe a single syllable of it but it was clear that he did.

"What happened to him then?" she asked. She had stopped making notes. She suspected that Frank Aston had

had a bad life, but in her experience, that all too often meant that the badness seeped in and was carried forever by the victim.

He looked sheepish. "Well, I'm not too sure . . ."

She presumed that Aston had been very deliberately vague in some areas, very deliberately mendacious in the rest. "He learned to drive, though," she suggested, as much to fill the time until Bayes got back with the truth. Which assumed that the name Frank Aston wasn't as fictitious as the rest of his biography.

"Oh, yes. I always insisted that all my drivers had driving licences that were as clean as a whistle."

I bet it was . . . And almost certainly a counterfeit . . .

"He got a job as a delivery driver, I recall, as soon as he learned to drive," he continued.

"What was the firm he worked for?"

"I'm not sure . . ." He frowned. "I'd have to check the paperwork. They gave him a glowing reference, though."

I'll bet they did.

"Where does he live?"

The frown deepened. "With me and the wife." His tone suggested that it was a stupid question.

"With you?"

He heard her surprise. "Oh, yes." He sighed contentedly. "He's become the son we never had, I suppose, although Fiona – Mrs Dunant – gets angry when I say that, although . . ." He lowered his voice. "I'm not sure that she's *really* angry."

"No?"

He shook his head. "No."

She was still trying to process the information that he had just given her. *Aston lived with the Dunants?*

"Do you have a picture of him?"

"I don't know . . ." He searched for his mobile, finding it in his breast pocket. He searched through it, finding a picture that satisfied him and showing it to her. A group of three; Henry Dunant, a woman of similar age and, between them, a much younger man; this last was fair-haired, a head taller than Dunant, blue-eyed, and clean-shaven.

"This him?"

"It is."

"Mind if I send it to my phone?"

He shrugged. "Go ahead."

She did so. Then, "Tell me about your nephew, Paul."

He made a face. "Paul? What about him?" If his demeanour had been almost soppy when discussing Frank Aston, it now hardened into utter contempt. This told her a lot, but she wanted more. "You don't like him?"

"He's a disgrace to the family."

"Why?"

"He was going to be a doctor. We were all so proud of him. His mum and dad were so chuffed . . ."

"And then he dropped out."

"That's right."

"So, he let you all down."

Dunant scowled. "I always said it contributed to the

death of my brother; he died of a stroke within the year. And *that* led to the death of Irene, his wife, not two months after that from a broken heart."

There was a knock on the door and Bayes' head appeared around it as it opened. "A word, sir?"

She stood, saying, "Excuse me, Mr Dunant."

"Of course, Inspector."

"I'll arrange for some tea to be sent in."

"That would be nice." He smiled broadly.

Outside the room, the corridor was cold but Bayes' information meant that she soon forgot the temperature.

"Frank Aston, aged thirty-one years. Father walked out when he was four, but his mother didn't waste time in finding a substitute. It was highly likely that said substitute also availed himself of Frank as well as his mother. Frank left home at the age of seventeen, and the mother's partner was stabbed to death shortly after."

"Would I be right in assuming that he was suspected, but not convicted?"

"You would."

"Anything on him after that?"

"He went on the game."

She raised her eyebrows. "Did he now?"

"Three convictions for soliciting in seven years. The last time he got a custodial sentence . . ."

There was something about his excitement that told her the answer to her next question. "Did he serve time in . . .?"

He nodded. "He was in Moorlands for five months."
He, at least, thought it highly significant. Was it a coincidence, though? Despite all she had said about coincidences, she was abruptly worried. Bayes had reassurance, though. "When he came out, he was homeless for three years."

"Would he have crossed paths with Warren or Kinison?"

"They would have all been there together for a month."

She hissed. "Shit . . ."

She had him.

There was a stentorian call along the corridor, "Wharton! Where the hell have you been? My office, five minutes."

Beverley closed her eyes, aware of Bayes' look of sympathy. She would have responded, but Lambert had already vanished around a corner.

She sighed. "According to Henry Dunant, Aston lives with him, which means he does his dirty work somewhere else. Get back in there and try to find out where that might be, while I waste my time in Lambert's office."

Chapter Forty-Six

"You went to the hospital."

"Sir . . ."

"I expressly told you not to, if you recall."

"Sir . . ."

"Do you recall that, Wharton?"

"Sir, if you'd let me . . ."

"Let you what? Do what you want? Ignore me? Ignore my rank?"

"No . . ."

"Christ, I know you're insubordinate, and I know you think I'm a waste of space, but this takes the biscuit."

She stood in front of the desk and listened to the clichés, mentally headbutting them back to him. She considered him really rather laughable, especially knowing what she knew. *I could let him ramble on, but . . .*

She had to consider John. Time was of the essence.

"Sir, that all might be correct, but it's essential I get back down to the interview room."

"What?"

"I know who our torso killer is." She had finally broken through his pathetically misplaced dignity.

"You know?"

". . . But I don't yet know *where* he is, which means I don't know where he's holding John Eisenmenger."

"Eisenmenger?"

She was moving to the door as she was speaking. "So, if you don't mind, we'll continue this *fascinating* conversation at some point in the future."

She left before he could speak again.

She met Bayes just as he was coming out of the interview room with Henry Dunant. He said, "We were just going to Mr Dunant's house to have a look at Frank's room."

In the car, with Dunant in the back, she said to Bayes, "What did you get?"

He kept his eyes on the road as he replied, "Nothing."

*

Fiona Dunant was very nice. She didn't mind in the least when her husband and Beverley and Bayes came into her house, didn't take off their shoes, and asked her a lot of questions. She kept smiling but not in a forced way. Around the dining room table, they sat and asked, "Where is Frank?"

"He had a couple of trips this morning – one to Oxford,

and one to Cheltenham. Since then, he's been on a half day. He mentioned going shopping."

"Where?"

She didn't know.

"Did he go in his Mercedes?"

"Oh, yes." Beverley look meaningfully at Bayes who nodded and left the room. "Where's he going?" demanded Fiona Dunant.

"He's making a call." Mrs Dunant looked at Beverley and might have pressed the point but Beverley continued, "What's your opinion of Frank, Mrs Dunant?"

She was as rotund as her husband but under the flesh and the make-up, Beverley judged that it was an attractive woman who replied, "He's a lovely lad."

"Polite?" Beverley tended to put witnesses and suspects into types; Mrs Dunant was already classified as the type to put a great deal of importance on politeness, just like her husband. Mrs Dunant nodded enthusiastically. "And he dresses so well!"

It was all that mattered, apparently. Bayes returned and received a stare from Fiona Dunant that he ignored.

She had made them tea, which she served in *Old Country Roses* cups. Beverley's was minutely chipped, she saw.

"How long has he lived with you?"

"Two, maybe three years. Ever since my husband employed him."

Beverley drank some tea. It was pretty good, she thought; as a rule, she didn't much care for the stuff, but this was passable. Mrs Dunant put down the cup, then looked across at her husband. He was nodding enthusiastically, Beverley observed.

He said, "That's right."

"Why are you here?" asked Fiona. "Is he in trouble?"

"No." Which was sort of true. Possibly, "not yet" would have been more accurate, or maybe even, "he will be shortly", but at the moment there was a degree of veracity in that single syllable.

"They want to eliminate him from their enquiries." Henry Dunant said, oh so helpfully. His wife looked as though she could guess what that meant.

"We need to look at his room."

"I'm not sure about that." Fiona looked at Henry as she said this, perhaps seeking his support, but finding none.

"We've got nothing to hide, and I'm sure Frank wouldn't mind . . ."

*

His bedroom was at the rear of the house. Henry Dunant said somewhat sadly, "When the girls all went their separate ways, the house felt empty. Frank moving in gave us a sense of renewal, if you know what I mean."

Neither Beverley nor Bayes did, but neither admitted it.

The room was neat and tidy and told them nothing. Beverley looked around while Bayes poked about in the built-in wardrobe and the bedside cabinet, and the Dunants looked on from the doorway. She peered under the neatly made bed, finding no body parts. She tried to visualise what the man who occupied this room might be like, and found it impossible. She asked the Dunants, "Does he have any friends?" It was a question born of frustration wedded to irritation. Frank Aston was an enigma to her. She would have to rely on finding his car, she judged, and that might be too late for John Eisenmenger.

"I don't think so." Henry Dunant sounded quite affronted by the suggestion.

"Oh, no," agreed his wife.

Bayes' phone rang. He left the room.

"What's his mobile number?" Beverley asked, hers in hand.

Henry shrugged. His wife said, "I'll have to go downstairs and fetch my phone. He's on speed dial, you see."

They went into the kitchen. Next to a big diary was her mobile; after a few moments in which she pressed buttons, she gave Beverley the number, who put it into her phone and called him. It went to voicemail. Bayes returned, shaking his head. Beverley smiled at the Dunants. "When Frank returns, tell him we'd like to talk to him, will you?"

"What about my car? It's at the station. I need it for my livelihood."

Mrs Dunant chipped in. "He's got an airport trip tonight."

"I'll arrange for you to be given a lift to the station as soon as possible."

"Can't I go with you?"

She was all apologies, "Normally, yes, but we're not going to the station, Mr Dunant."

In the car, Bayes said, "Nothing on the Merc, but I've asked that everyone keeps an eye open for it."

"It'll be in a lock-up somewhere; out of sight."

"What do we do now?"

"We go back to the station where you get the records for this number." She sent it to his phone.

"Aston's?"

She nodded.

Chapter Forty-Seven

If John Eisenmenger had thought that he was incapable of taking more pain, the taxi driver had proved otherwise by applying a lit cigarette to the back of his neck. As Eisenmenger had screamed, he had done nothing. He had stayed silently behind the chair, and through the agony, Eisenmenger saw in the mirror that his torturer had been breathing in the screams, the pain, the distress; he had had a look of pleasure on his face, as if he were listening to Mozart or an intricate Bach concerto. Every one of Eisenmenger's screams had been to him something to savour.

The screams had come out of Eisenmenger despite the pain in his fractured ribs and the dull throbbing of his head. Eisenmenger hadn't cared about the rib fractures at that moment. The screams had come long and loud and lustily and, if at the end of every one he felt his ribs grate, he didn't care because of the torment from his neck, and because of the smell of burning flesh – *his* burning flesh – that came with the smoke that curled around his head.

And, when he had stopped screaming, there had been no sound for a long time from the taxi driver. It was almost as if he were no longer there, as if it were a wraith that was reflected in the mirror opposite. Eisenmenger panted, making the panting as shallow as possible, Eventually, he asked breathlessly, "What are you waiting for?" He hurt everywhere, it seemed to him.

Still no sound from anywhere in the room.

Eisenmenger wanted to talk but he was aware that every word he said was somehow giving this man power. He said no more. His reward was the striking of a match, breath sucked through a cigarette that he couldn't see, and then intense agony again as the cigarette was stubbed into the back of his neck once more.

He screamed again, of course.

The taxi driver came around to the front of him. He stood and looked at the trolley with all its instruments so neatly arrayed as Eisenmenger sobbed. He pursed his lips; he put down the packet of cigarettes, then pointed at a razor blade, his head on one side. He picked up a vial; it contained viscous but clear fluid. With a sly smile, he looked at Eisenmenger as he sobbed in pain, and said, "Maybe the nitric acid next time. What do you think, John?"

Chapter Forty-Eight

"Look at this." Bayes seemed excited.

Long years of experience had taught Beverley that a case progressed from excitement to frustration and back again many times before its end, and sometimes that end was never reached. "What?"

"The phone records of Frank Aston."

"What about them?"

"He had a close friend, it would seem. Certainly, he phoned him a lot."

"Who?"

"Paul Dunant."

*

It was busy in the Emergency Department. Peter Sulston was stitching a long cut on an old man's leg caused by falling through a glass cold frame, and Beverley and Bayes had to wait what seemed an inordinately long time before they could speak to him. They told the sister in charge in the Emergency Department who they were and she went into the curtained-off cubicle to tell him of their presence, but he wasn't going to be hurried. When he at last appeared, his face told Beverley all she needed to know about his mood. He looked as if his expression had been chiselled out of stone as he went first to a sink, washed his hands, then proceeded to a desk, where he wrote something in a medical record that appeared on a screen in front of him. A nurse whispered something to him, but he kept his eyes on the screen. Beverley approached him. "Doctor Sulston?"

He looked up. "What is it?"

"Can we go to your office?"

"Can't this wait? You can see how hectic this place is."

"No, it can't."

He made a noise out of the back of his throat. "Five minutes. That's all I can spare."

"That's all we need." In truth, she didn't know how long they would need, but she didn't give a shit.

He stood and led them to his office. On their way, Bayes' phone rang and he hung back as Beverley and Sulston walked on. They arrived, and this time she let him sit behind his own desk. "What's this about?"

"Paul."

"He's off duty."

"Since when?"

"He went off duty about two hours ago."

"Where is he? Did he go to your home?"

"I don't know. I'm not his keeper."

"He's your partner, right?"

He became instantly wary. "We live together," he agreed cautiously.

"Is it a legal arrangement?"

"If you mean, is it a civil partnership, then no."

"Does the name Frank Aston mean anything to you?"

"No." But it did, she could see it in his eyes, his face, his whole demeanour.

"You're sure?"

Sulston looked directly into her eyes. A mistake, if he was still trying to deceive her, but she saw that he was being pushed slowly to the truth. It was a calculation that she had observed many times; the rebalancing of priorities and reassessment of affinities. "A friend of his, I think . . . He's mentioned him a few times."

"Are there occasions when you don't know where he is?"

He bridled, "Of course there are."

"You've no idea where he goes on those occasions?"

She saw bright lights were being shone into the corners of his whole life and that he was seeing things that he hadn't known – perhaps hadn't wanted to know – were there. The capacity of human beings for self-deception was incredible, she knew. He said quietly, "No," but he had dropped his head.

"No idea at all?"

"None."

She smiled. "Let me tell you what's going on, Doctor Sulston."

"Going on?" he asked. There was a touch of panic about his words.

"You've heard about the bodies that have recently been showing up?"

"Tramps, or something . . ." Nothing to do with him.

"They were dismembered and beheaded. Before that they were tortured, we think."

He looked suitably aghast. "That wasn't in the papers . . ."

"Nevertheless, it's what happened, and we think that a man called Frank Aston may have done it."

His voice was agonised as he asked in a low voice, "But why?"

Beverley looked at him with contempt. "Christ only knows. That's not the point."

Sulston had to ask what the point was, even though she guessed that he already had a small but dreadful inkling about the truth. She said, "And it's possible that your 'partner', Paul, might have been helping him, Doctor Sulston."

"No, surely not . . ."

"Not definitely, no, but we need to talk to him. And if you shield him, and it turns out that he was involved, Doctor Sulston, your position isn't going to save you."

The pause that followed was long and during it Sulston kept his head low. Beverley waited. Bayes returned but

Sulston didn't react as the door opened. When Bayes looked as though he was going to say something, she silently but angrily waved him to silence. This was crucial, she knew. He sat down quietly. At last, Sulston looked up at her. She could see the calculations that had been going on in his head, and could also see that he knew that, when it came down to it, he had no choice.

She asked after a precisely timed delay, "Do you have any idea where we might find Paul?"

"His parents' old house. I think he goes there a lot. I always thought it was . . ."

"Where? Where is it?"

"The city centre."

"Have you got an address?"

"Followill Avenue. Number thirty-two, I think."

Chapter Forty-Nine

Eisenmenger's mind was fractured. The pain from the burns in his neck, the stabs of agony that came with every breath, the soreness of the raw flesh at his wrists and ankles, the dull ache in his head and the throbbing of his knee were a background for the fear and paranoia that had grown within him, while the unpleasantness of sitting naked in his own urine, and the looming sense of despondent hopelessness, crushed him. He was done. Had he had something to tell the man who had done it to him, he would have gladly spoken, but there was nothing to say, no secrets to spill.

The thought of the acid and what it might do to him would not go away.

The stress, he told himself, came from the inescapability of his situation.

It didn't help.

He could only wait, in pain, for more pain to come.

*

In the car as they headed for the city centre at speed, Bayes said, "Dunant's been raising hell. Said we promised him a lift to get his car back from the station, or something."

"Shit! Forgot. Arrange for . . ."

"I've sorted it."

She glanced at him and twitched a smile. "Thanks, Sergeant."

"And there are three backup cars on the way to Followill Avenue . . ."

"Make sure that they park up out of sight of the house."

"They know what to do." His tone was brim full of confidence and she saw him anew. He might be green but he was smart; perhaps he would work out all right . . .

She glanced at him. *Shame you're gay*.

They drove on.

It was a small house in the middle of a terrace in Followill Avenue, which was a road lined by lime trees, behind which were similar terraces that curved gently down to the docks. It was dirty and uncared for; it looked empty, and probably was for much of the time. One of thousands in the city centre, where people lived and died, procreated, got drunk, laughed and cried, fell and picked themselves up, sometimes elevating themselves to a higher place, often falling even lower. It was a place she knew well; or, at least, a type of place she knew well. It was also a type of place she hated. Here, was criminality, here was sadness, here was distress. Here was the source of so much that she hated.

And yet, this? Here? It didn't seem possible to her. This was a place of petty malice, not the Grand Guignol that headless, limbless torsos represented. The families that lived around here stole and fenced and beat each other up, they forged MOT certificates and fly-tipped and defrauded the HMRC. That also around here there could be torture and death and pain, seemed impossible, given the proximity of the houses, the feeling of claustrophobia, and the sense of crowding.

A police car was parked up out of sight at either end of the street, the third at the back of the house, having driven down an alleyway. It was this third that Beverley joined first. She and Bayes peered over the back fence into an overgrown garden. One of the uniforms – she'd forgotten his name – said, "The neighbours over there have repeatedly complained about the state of the garden."

She could see the garden to the left was neatly tended with a small vegetable patch, a greenhouse and small patio. The contrast with the grubby, litter-strewn jungle that was at the back of the house of interest was stark. It was so dense that they couldn't actually see the back of the house very well. Bayes asked, "What do they know about their neighbours?"

"They thought it was just empty. The windows are boarded up."

"No lights? No sounds?"

The uniform shook his head. "Not those."

"What does that mean?"

"They also complained about the drains . . ."

"Why doesn't that surprise me?" Bayes murmured.

Beverley asked, "What about the other side? Who lives there?"

The uniform sniggered. "The Bosts."

"The Bosts? They live here?"

He nodded. Bayes asked, "Who are we talking about?"

"The Bosts are old friends of ours," she replied. "I think Kevin got out last year, didn't he? What was it, two years? For handling, wasn't it?"

The uniform – Simpson, she recalled at that moment – nodded and said, "Sentenced to four, out in two."

"And his sons are taking their places in the family business," she explained to Bayes. "They're a family firm that's growing."

She looked down the alleyway. To Simpson she ordered, "Stay here. You probably won't be needed, but you never know."

They climbed back into the car and drove slowly around to a second police car that blocked one end of Followill Avenue. Here, she spoke with Constable Pearson. "Anything?"

"Not from the house. We've had a bit of stick from people who want to go down the road."

Bayes said in a low voice to her, "Sir?" She heard a warning note in the word.

269

She turned. She spotted at once the reason for it. Lambert had arrived, driven by Frazier. She straightened up as he got out of the car, not sure what to expect. He said, "Where are we at, DCI?"

"One car at either end of the road and one in the alley at the back. Vans are on the way."

"Armed Response Unit?"

"We've no evidence that they're armed. We'll just take Tasers."

He looked at her for an appraising moment. Was he going to argue? She hoped not.

"And you think Eisenmenger's in there?"

"I think that's where all of the men in the torso case were killed. I suspect that Eisenmenger was taken and may well be in there."

"You'd better get some ambulances on standby, then."

It was good advice and she was grateful for it. She nodded at Bayes, who hurried off. She called, "Make sure they don't use sirens, Bayes."

He waved a hand but didn't look back. She was left with her commanding officer. This wasn't the Lambert she was used to. She didn't quite know how to deal with it. She said, "Any other advice, sir?"

He had been watching Bayes but when she said this, he almost jerked, as if shocked. "Be careful."

She thought it lame, but well intentioned.

Bayes returned. Lambert asked him, "All set?"

"They're on their way, sir."

A police van arrived and four big police officers got out. Beverley and Bayes lined up with them to take out helmets and bulletproof vests from the back of the van. When they had put them on, she turned back to Lambert. "What are you waiting for?" he asked.

She heard the pronoun and fully appreciated its significance; deep down, Lambert hadn't changed.

Chapter Fifty

The door began to open and Eisenmenger found himself stiffening instinctively.

This is it. This is where the pain really starts.

He tried to stop such thoughts, but they kept coming. He tried not to look at himself in the mirror, but saw a terrified old man.

Oh, God. Acid . . . The agony . . . The disfigurement . . . The smell . . . For the first time in his life, he found himself wishing for – longing for – death. The prospect of oblivion seemed so sweet . . .

It wasn't the taxi driver who came in.

It was the porter from the hospital. What was his name? He couldn't break through the pain to reach his memory. His voice was dry and his tongue huge and cracked as he said, "I know you . . ."

"Hello, John. You don't look well."

Eisenmenger's eyes were sore and his vision was bleary; so much of him hurt, though, that this didn't register too high in the scale of things. He felt light-headed at one moment, nailed to the ground in the next. He knew where he was, he didn't have the faintest idea of what had happened to him. He remembered, he forgot; the room was still, the room swirled, or it heaved, or it retreated from him . . .

The porter walked towards him. "I'm truly sorry."

The sound of his footsteps was loud, his voice was soft; Eisenmenger felt cold. He shivered. He tried to raise his head but the pain of the burns on his neck deterred him. "What for?" He knew it was a stupid question, but that was *all* he knew. He wasn't capable of framing another sentence, another enquiry. His bladder leaked and, due to dehydration, it stank horribly, and stung the reddened flesh of the backs of his legs, but he was barely aware of it.

The porter, though, grimaced. "I could have saved you all this."

This time, Eisenmenger *did* look up, the pain from the burns stabbing him but the words had somehow got through. "You could?" he croaked.

The porter held up a glass vial but Eisenmenger couldn't focus on it properly. "What's that?" His tongue tried unsuccessfully to wet his lips.

Without replying to this, he put the vial in his pocket, but did so with a flourish, as if he were a stage magician trying to misdirect the audience. He shook his head. "You do look a mess, John." His voice was all earnestness and sorrow. "Frank doesn't care, as I do."

Eisenmenger tried to focus on the porter but his eyes wouldn't play ball. "Frank?" he asked, his voice barely a whisper.

"He doesn't concern himself with the aesthetics of it all, you see."

There was a long pause as Eisenmenger took a deep breath which stopped abruptly as the pain bit in. The porter went to the trolley. Eisenmenger saw him do this through eyes that were slits. "Is that it? Do you use the acid?"

He looked up at Eisenmenger, his face showing surprise. "Me? Acid?" He shivered. "Good God, no."

Another breath as deep as he could make it. "Then, why . . .?"

"I'm sorry?"

Breathe in again but not too deeply. Once, twice, thrice . . .

"Why are you here?" he asked. From somewhere, Eisenmenger was genuinely interested.

The porter frowned. "Because I know you. We met in the hospital, didn't we?"

Eisenmenger remembered that, he was sure. "Yes . . . You took me to the café."

The other nodded. "That's right. I liked you."

Eisenmenger peered at him. "Liked me?" His voice was hoarse and soft. He didn't understand. He didn't understand anything at all; at times now, he didn't understand diddly-squat. Even the right way up was becoming a bit tricky, he was now discovering, what with the pain and the despair and the degradation.

"Have you come to save me?" He tried to sound cynical, couldn't tell if he had succeeded.

"I tried that already. It didn't work."

"Why are you here, then?"

"I thought you'd be pleased to see me before the end."

Shallow breaths . . . "Oh, I am, I am."

He picked up the small glass bottle that contained the nitric acid and tilted it, eyeing it closely. "Are you? Really?"

"Believe me."

He put down the bottle. A smile twitched across his face and sighed. "That's a shame, John. A real shame."

The door to the room opened behind him. The taxi driver came in. The porter turned. They looked at each other, moved together and kissed, a thing of real passion, a thing of love that, in this dark place of torture, was horrible for Eisenmenger to see. They parted and the taxi driver said to his lover, "Leave us alone now, Paul. I'll call you when I need you."

Paul, that was it . . .

The porter turned to Eisenmenger. "Sorry," he whispered. He walked to the door and left them alone.

The taxi driver smiled at Eisenmenger. "Where were we? The acid, wasn't it?"

And Eisenmenger braced himself to die in terrible pain.

The door burst open, allowing in the sound of battering. The porter shouted, "They're here, Frank."

Frank could see that Paul was terrified. He had been increasingly worried by Paul recently. He had seen that his heart was no longer in the Great Project, that he had been perhaps looking for a way out. His terror in this situation was perhaps justified, he supposed, but as he looked now at his partner in this grand enterprise, he saw only someone who wanted out.

"You go." He spoke sadly but with huge tenderness. It was all up for them now. He didn't know how it had happened, but he was nothing if not a realist.

"What about you?"

Frank shrugged. He looked down at the man in the chair. "I'll think of something."

"We should stay together."

Frank's face didn't change. "It's over, Paul." His voice was flat.

They heard movement from outside. Frank picked up the vial of acid and moved around to the back of the man in the chair. He looked meaningfully at Paul and then jerked his head backwards. "Go."

Still he hesitated.

"Go, Paul. *Now.*"

As he moved past him, Paul grabbed hold of his hand for a moment. They embraced, then kissed, mouth to mouth. They let go, and he went to the blacked out, padded window. He raised the sash, stepped through so that he sat on the sill. Having looked back at his partner, he launched himself off it.

Frank put the vial on the floor, then closed the window.

He returned to Eisenmenger, picked up the vial, then waited patiently.

Chapter Fifty-One

The door had come down easily with the aid of two burly
police officers and a metal battering ram. Beverley was first
through, though, but only because she always felt she should
be. They broke through into a small house that might have
been normally occupied; clean carpet, knick-knacks on the
hall table, a pendulum clock on the wall, even a smell of
home cooking.

Surely, I haven't made a mistake?

There were stairs on the left that led upwards; there were
open doorways to the right and straight on. She stood to
one side to let the grunts do the work, whilst she and Bayes
waited in the hallway not looking at each other. In her ear,
Lambert barked, "What's happening?"

"Nothing at the moment."

He growled as if this would magic something out of

nothing. There was a call from the back room. "Sir? You'd best come in here."

She walked quickly to join whoever it was who had called her. One of the burlies from the van; he looked sick. He stood aside to reveal an empty room in which there was a huge wood-burning stove. The only other thing in the room was a large black plastic bin of some kind – a coal bunker? But surely that should have been outside . . . Then she saw it. The front window of the stove was heavily covered in soot but she could still see a partially burned head inside it.

"Shit," she breathed.

"Look in the bunker."

She didn't want to but she knew that she had to. She reached out a gloved hand and lifted the lid. It contained not coal, nor wood logs, but arms, legs and heads. A stink rose from it. She quickly dropped the lid, looking around.

At least there's no doubt we're in the right place . . .

But where is John?

She beckoned the man out of the room and they reconvened in the hallway. She looked around.

Upstairs? They'd need a soundproof room, wouldn't they? Is there a basement?

She asked in a whisper of everyone and no one in particular, "Does anyone know these houses?"

Two of them did.

"Do they have basements?"

No.

"Upstairs, then."

She led the way up the carpeted staircase. They moved slowly and as quietly as they could, but to Beverley's ears their sheer number and the bulkiness of their clothes meant that they made a fuck of a lot of rustling and creaking, not to mention over-heavy breathing. At the top was a landing with four doorways leading off it; only one was open. She could see that there was a bathroom beyond.

She turned, trod lightly on the carpet and listened intently. The others came up behind her and she told them curtly and silently to stop moving so that she could hear the better. Nothing.

What now?

One would lead to a small box room . . . *Not in there.*

Front or back bedroom?

The back, I think.

She walked swiftly to the door on her right, next to the box room, pushed open the door . . .

And walked into hell.

Chapter Fifty-Two

The door opened and Eisenmenger saw a woman he didn't recognise until she gasped and said, "John?" in a voice that he knew so well. He opened his mouth, but could only croak. He was too dry, too sore.

The taxi driver was behind him. He saw reflected in the mirror that he held a vial at an angle over his head. He heard him say, "This is concentrated nitric acid."

He looked up. The stopper was off. The hand was trembling. He looked down very quickly.

*

Beverley entered a darkened room, predominantly red. The floor felt soft; the walls *looked* soft. John Eisenmenger, very naked and looking very ill, sat in wooden chair; no, he was *shackled* to it. And behind him, stood a youngish man — fairish hair that looked greasy and lank, blue eyes that didn't suit him, a pinched face and tight mouth. *Frank Aston*. He had a small glass bottle tilted above John's head. There was clear liquid within, it looked thick and turgid. A vapour rose lazily from it and she believed that it was evil.

She held up her hand to stop everyone else from entering the room. Bayes was already inside, but the rest of the team remained on the landing outside.

"What do you want?" she asked, trying to sound unconcerned. She had to be clinical about it, she knew.

"What do you fucking think?"

"To get away?" she guessed. *Sound sympathetic.*

"A banana for the lady!" It was a lunatic speaking, she thought. He added, "How many outside?"

"Four."

"And in the street?"

She hesitated.

He tilted the bottle that he held above Eisenmenger's head a little more. The liquid moved very close to its lip. "In the street? How many?"

"I don't know exactly," she supplied, hoping that he would believe her ignorance. "There's at least one car at either end of the street."

"Tell them to fuck off."

"What?" She knew what he meant, but she wanted time to think.

"Tell them to get out of there."

"Even if I do, it won't help, will it? That poor fucker's not going anywhere, is he?"

"You mean, John?" He spoke slyly and was grinning.

"Yes, John. You're not going to be able to take him with you as a hostage."

She saw him look down at John Eisenmenger.

"You know," he murmured thoughtfully, "You're right."

Frank's mind had been splintered for a long time. He was well used to the feeling of weightlessness and disorientation that accompanied a hop from one splinter to the next; he felt that now. He was tired of the game and tired of the slaughter; he was tired, full stop. The bitch was right. He couldn't get out now; he couldn't run, and he didn't want to. He just wanted to hurt something . . .

He tipped the bottle a little more.

A drop of fluid hung on the lip of the vial, clinging to it, a thing of menacing, smoky beauty. He stared into it. Below it was the man in the chair; a thing of ugliness. The thing looked up, then very quickly down. He might have whimpered. He bowed his head and tried to move out of the way of what was going to happen to him. He was a fool, Frank thought. No one escapes fate.

Frank was transfixed by what he could do . . .

Bayes moved swiftly. He threw himself to the side, in front of the open door, and fired his Taser. The needles fired forward, their silver wires unfurling behind them. They hit Frank Aston in the chest.

The drop fell from the bottle onto Eisenmenger just before the Taser needles hit. He began to scream.

Frank Aston jerked uncontrollably as ten thousand

volts passed through him. The bottle was jerked from his fingers. The acid splashed across his face. He, too, began to scream as he fell to the floor, his voice jerking as his body jerked.

Chapter Fifty-Three

Bayes returned home. Adrian was used to his partner coming in late, but he wasn't used to the mood of utter despondency and melancholy that he brought with him that evening. He was in the kitchen, preparing lasagne and called out, "Tom? I'm in here."

Bayes entered but Adrian didn't look at him. Bayes went to the fridge and pulled out a beer without saying anything. He opened the can and took a long, deep draught. Only then did Adrian look round. "What's wrong?"

Bayes began to cry and Adrian went to him. Bayes put down the can as Adrian held out his arms, a look of deep concern on his face. He held his partner tightly; at first Bayes remained stiff, but after a few minutes, he slowly relaxed and returned the hug. Then his tears flowed freely.

"What's the matter?"

But the words wouldn't come at once; only after Adrian

had led him to the sitting room and they were side by side, Bayes with his head back, looking up at nothing, did he explain.

"I blinded a man today."

"Oh, my God . . ."

"I'm suspended pending an investigation . . ." Adrian didn't know what to say. There was nothing he *could* say. Tom added, "I think I might resign anyway, Adrian."

Chapter Fifty-Four

Eisenmenger had a side room this time, not that he was aware of much for the first day. The second day was one of pain, despite the regular morphine infusions from a dosage regulator by his bed. Only during the third day did Eisenmenger become sufficiently compos mentis to start to make sense both to himself and to the nurses who were looking after him, chief among whom resided under the name Sister Alfreda Berrigan which, only on day four did he come to appreciate, was a magnificent moniker.

She came into his room on that morning, asking as she always did, "How are you today, Doctor Eisenmenger?"

He sat up in the uncomfortable bed for the first time, an action that made him suddenly aware of all the places that he hurt, as well as the drips that entered into the back of each hand and the crook of his left elbow. "Better."

"Good." She beamed and he could believe that she really wanted him to be better, and perhaps not just because she needed the bed. "I must do your readings."

These were completed after five minutes, but she said, "Your temperature's still up."

"Is it this?" He indicated the adhesive bandage that covered the wound across his chest; he was vaguely aware that when the dressing had been changed yesterday, the yellow-green of pus had stained the under-surface of the old bandage.

"Perhaps. You've had a bit of a UTI too, and the CT scan of your chest showed probable patchy consolidation that the radiologist was concerned about."

He was constipated, too; he knew that sooner rather than later, it would become a priority, but for today he hoped it could wait.

She said, "Have you opened your bowels yet?" When he didn't reply, she said, "We'll do something about it. I'll get the doctor to write you up for some laxative."

He was under the care of Dr Judith Buck, an acute medicine physician. She came in with Alfreda after he had breakfasted on two Weetabix, an overripe banana and tea made with full fat milk that made him feel nauseous. After the meal, he felt no better, perhaps slightly worse.

"How's it going?" she enquired. He knew that if there was one place on earth he could – should – answer that question truthfully, it was here, yet he still felt compelled to say untruthfully, "Not too bad."

She looked at his notes on her tablet. "Your kidney function's improving."

"Good."

"But your white count's still up."

"Bad."

She looked at him. "But you feel better?"

He nodded. "A bit."

She leaned towards him, peering at him. It was the exact antithesis of sexual intimacy. She asked, "May I?"

May she what? He didn't know. She reached out with both hands to his shoulders and pulled him gently forward. Her grip was firm. It didn't matter that she was gentle, the cut across his chest still protested, and his fractured ribs still shouted at him. She had cherry nail polish, he saw, trying to keep his mind off the pain. Her blouse was dark green, her slacks black. She was a tall woman, with dark hair cut in a short bob. She was wearing a scent he recognised but couldn't name. "I need to see those cigarette burns and where the acid splashed you."

He at last comprehended. He put his chin on his chest. She murmured, "They're all right."

She allowed him to lean back on the pillows.

"May I see the backs of your thighs? They were badly inflamed."

"Is there no dignity for a patient? I'm not used to this."

Alfreda stepped forward. "I'll help you." She pressed a button so that the bed went flat, then rolled him. She, too, was gentle, but it still hurt him. Peering at the backs of legs and his buttocks, Judith Buck said, "Good. They're not infected."

He was rolled back and, his dignity restored, the bed head was raised.

"You can go home as soon as the bloods normalise and your temperature comes down."

"It can't happen too soon for me, Doctor Buck. Alfreda's kind ministrations notwithstanding."

"The police have been asking to see you."

"And?"

"I've suggested this afternoon. Okay?"

Before a lunch that he wasn't anticipating with much relish, Claire Woodforde came to see him. "I came a couple of days ago, but you were asleep and I couldn't stay."

"I'm sorry . . ."

"No need to apologise." She smiled. He thought it a sad thing to behold. She added quickly, "I'm leaving the infirmary."

"Really?" He was genuinely surprised. "Why?"

"Oh . . ." There was a silence. He didn't feel the need to fill it; perhaps this was the morphine, or the antibiotics. Eventually, she added, "Matthew found a new job."

It was a lie, but he didn't point out what they both knew.

After a lunch that spectacularly lived down to his expectations – macaroni cheese, orange juice and a pot of cold rice pudding with jam – Beverley and Phelps came into the room. She wrinkled her nose at the remnants of the meal on the tray by his bed but said nothing. There were two hard plastic chairs and a high-backed chair covered in unnaturally slippery faux leather; they chose the hard plastic. Eisenmenger murmured, "Make yourselves comfortable, if you can."

"What is it with visitors' chairs in hospitals?" demanded Phelps. "All I remember from when my missus was in for a gall bladder op is how hard they were."

Eisenmenger said, "If you had to eat the food, you'd only remember that, believe me."

Beverley asked, "How are you, John?"

"Fairly shitty. I can't work out whether it's real or just being in this place."

Phelps looked around. "Being in this place, I should think."

"With any luck, I'll be out soon."

"We need a statement, John."

"And I thought you were just here for me." Which at least embarrassed Phelps.

It bounced off Beverley, though. "Think again, Doctor."

"Where's Bayes?" asked Eisenmenger.

Beverley and Phelps exchanged glances before she said, "Taking some time off."

Eisenmenger accepted this lie. "Can't say I blame him."

"However, the job must go on and you're a key witness."

"To be honest, I'm not sure how much use I'll be. One of them – the taxi driver – didn't identify himself, and the other one – the hospital porter – I only heard referred to as 'Paul'. No second name."

Phelps noted this down.

"But you'll be able to identify the one called Paul?"

"I guess."

"That's all we'll need."

"What about the other one? Perhaps I could identify him."

Beverley glanced at Phelps, who dropped his head. "Perhaps," she replied quietly.

Eisenmenger didn't pick up on what had just happened. He asked, "So, who were they?"

Before Phelps could say anything, Beverley pointed out, "*After* you've made and signed a statement, Doctor Eisenmenger."

Chapter Fifty-Five

He had been home only a few hours the next day when Beverley rang the doorbell. She had with her two bottles of champagne. Holding them up, she said, "They're chilled. I'll put one in the fridge." She waved him out of the way and went into the depths of the house. He followed and arrived just as she was shutting the door of the refrigerator. She turned back to the other bottle that she had put on the drainer next to the sink. As she unwrapped the foil, he asked, "Is this all in aid of my recovery?"

"And the end of the case. Frank Aston and Paul Dunant were charged on multiple counts yesterday."

She undid the wire cage, then expertly twisted out the cork without a sound. "Glasses?" she asked. He found some and she poured.

He asked, "Multiple counts of what?"

"Murder, kidnapping, grievous bodily harm . . . You

name it, they've been charged with it." She ushered him into the sitting room. She looked around. "Nice and tidy."

"Dennis and Jeremy," he sighed. "Bless them. I think they see me as a son . . . or perhaps a pet. Anyway, they looked after the place in my absence."

"I met Dennis. Seemed a nice chap."

"Not your type."

"I got that impression."

He held up his glass. "You realise this stuff is going to play havoc with my medication."

"Oh . . ."

He took a deep draught. "Fuck it . . ."

She laughed. "How are you, by the way?" She couldn't sound too concerned, he knew. It was how their relationship worked. He sometimes wished it were otherwise.

"The fractured ribs are going to take weeks. These . . ." He opened out his arms and legs so that the bandages on his wrists and arms peeped out from underneath his clothes. ". . . Are healing nicely, as is everything else, thanks to the drugs."

She took the glass from him. "You won't want any more, I take it?"

He laughed and took it back. "You can piss off."

They drank in silence for a while, side by side on the sofa. She took off her jacket. Her peach-coloured tee shirt said, *You don't like pork? Get stuffed* . . . "This is good," he said as they put their glasses down. "Thanks."

"My pleasure." She put her head back, her eyes closed.

He put out his hand to hers; she didn't pull away. After another deliciously long pause, he murmured, "I heard a rumour in hospital."

She was instantly nervous. "What was it?"

"That Frank Aston was blinded." When she didn't respond, he looked directly at her. "Is that true?"

She held his gaze. "He played with acid, John. He hurt you and he hurt others with it."

"So it *is* true."

"When Tom hit him with the Taser, he splashed the acid on his face . . ."

"Shit . . ."

"Tom was devastated."

"I bet he was."

"It's automatic suspension and investigation by the IPCC, as well." Her tone was full of anger, he heard. "I'm afraid it'll finish him."

"Poor bastard." She didn't know whether he was referring to Bayes or Aston. She didn't dare ask.

They didn't speak for a while until he said softly, "I don't understand."

"You?" she replied dreamily. "I never thought I'd hear you say that."

"Why the arm in the waste bin and the head on the roof?"

"That was Paul. He said he wanted an end to it, but didn't dare confront Frank directly. Frank's mad. At the end, Frank scared the shit out of him."

"Yet Frank helped him to get away."

"Frank was loyal, I'll give him that."

"Loyal, but completely insane."

She laughed. "Paul *tried* to get away, anyway. He might have succeeded, if we hadn't got the back alleyway covered."

They drank and she got up and fetched the bottle because he was still sore in all sorts of places. After she had refilled their glasses and they had drunk some more, he said, "What about the hospital deaths, Beverley?"

"What about them?"

"Do you think they were connected? Paul worked at the hospital, after all . . ."

"Quite possibly, but proving it's another thing, especially as Doctor Sulston's not cooperating."

He examined the bubbles in the glass and didn't say anything for a while. Then, "He showed me a small glass ampoule."

"Who?"

"The porter. Paul."

"What sort of ampoule?"

He thought as deeply as he could. "I don't know, I couldn't see it properly. It looked like the kind of thing that drugs come in. You know, a glass ampoule."

"So . . . What?" She looked at him, an expression of concern. "You think he stole it from the hospital?"

"I got the impression that he could have used it on me – injected it into me somehow – he would have done."

"Why would he do that?"

"To save me from Frank, possibly. You said he was having doubts . . ."

"But you can't recall what precisely this ampoule had in it?"

He shook his head. "No."

"Then it's not enough."

"No?"

"A defence lawyer would have a field day with it. You were practically delirious when we found you. You were in renal failure and intense pain from all that had been done to you, and you can't recall what was written on the side of the ampoule."

He couldn't argue.

They finished the bottle. It was getting dark outside. He yawned just as his phone chimed. He looked at it and groaned softly.

"What is it?" asked Beverley.

"It's from the production company. Another script for editing."

"Is it that hard?"

He looked at her. "You'd be surprised how much crap they put in. People seem to think that pathologists are capable of incredible things when it comes to solving crimes."

"If only they knew the truth . . ." Her tone was sly.

He stared at her for a beat before saying affectionately, "Fuck off."

Laughing, she said, "At least it's money, John."

"There is that," he agreed with a smile.

She said then thoughtfully, "We could open the second bottle and take it upstairs . . ."

He looked at her.

"I'm not up to . . ."

"No." She smiled and then touched him lightly on the face. "I didn't think you were." Her voice was soft and full of affection.

Chapter Fifty-Six

The days healed him and healed him well. They also afforded him much time to think about what had happened at the hospital. He returned many times to the notes he had made concerning the hospital deaths. He tried to make an appointment to see the CEO of the infirmary, Gary Benson.

"May I ask what it's about, Doctor Eisenmenger?" The voice at the end of the phone line was low and warm.

"About Paul Durant."

Although still low, the voice was abruptly cold. "You're not in contact with the press, are you?"

"Not at all." Then he added, as if it would help, "I met him a while ago."

This was met with silence. As silences went, it was cold and distant. He kept his voice light as he said, "If I can't talk to Mr Benson, I may have to go to the press, though."

"I'll see what I can do."

The phone went completely dead; he didn't know whether to ring off or not. He decided to keep holding. After a couple of minutes, she came back on the line. Her tone was completely different; now it was openly hostile. "He can see you this afternoon, Doctor Eisenmenger. At five-thirty."

He wasn't asked if this was convenient. He accepted it.

Once again, it wasn't just Eisenmenger and another, but a threesome. Once again, it seemed as if Benson and Greeley acted as a double act. They sat together as Eisenmenger was ushered into the room by the same personal assistant as before, although this time she seemed to him to be distinctly frostier; perhaps it was his imagination.

"Please, sit down, Doctor Eisenmenger." It was Greeley who spoke, as if he were in charge; perhaps he was. Benson was only the CEO, so often the figurehead and nothing more.

After he had sat at the table opposite the two men, Greely went on, "You wanted to talk about Paul Dunant."

"A porter who was employed at the trust."

"We're in the process of terminating his employment following the recent disclosures . . ."

Benson just stared at him. His gaze was piercing and disconcerting. Eisenmenger tried to concentrate on Greeley; not that he was a particularly prepossessing sight. He replied, "You know his history, don't you?"

"His employment history, you mean? The Human Resources Department will have . . ."

"He lived with Peter Sulston."

Benson looked nonplussed; Greeley smiled. "What's your point?"

"Peter Sulston protected him when he was a medical student at Imperial College."

"I wouldn't know about that."

"There was some funny business with controlled drugs. Paul Dunant was asked to leave."

"What has this to do with us?"

"It was only after the intervention of Doctor Sulston that the affair was laid to rest."

"If you have any suspicions that the affair was not correctly dealt with, you need to speak to them, not us."

"But Peter Sulston and Paul Dunant have been working here. Practically in the same department."

"You're not implying that Doctor Sulston was involved in that dreadful affair, are you? I'm sure that he would take a very dim view of anyone saying such a slanderous thing in public, as would the trust."

"I'm not."

"Good," Benson said. Greeley said nothing, but his expression as he regarded Eisenmenger struck the pathologist as hostile.

Eisenmenger said, "Claire Woodforde's leaving. Is that correct?"

"What of it?"

"Is she being forced out?"

"Why on earth would you think that?"

"Because she's made a nuisance of herself."

Greeley and Benson looked at each other; Eisenmenger couldn't fathom the significance of it. Benson said, "Doctor Woodforde resigned for personal reasons, I understand."

"Nothing to do with her obsession with the excess of deaths?"

"Nothing."

"She wasn't hounded out?"

"What the hell does that mean?" asked Greeley although, Eisenmenger noted, Benson seemed oddly subdued.

"Nobody came to the trust executive and suggested that it would be best if she left?"

"Of course not."

"Not Doctor Sulston?"

"No."

"I don't believe you. I think that it's very convenient for you to have Doctor Woodforde leave, so that you can forget all about her theories and look elsewhere for a cause of the excess deaths."

"I see that you've also become obsessed with them." Greeley's tone mocked him.

"Doesn't the excess worry you?"

Benson nearly exploded. "Of course it does!" he said vehemently. "I'd be in gross dereliction of my duty if I ignored it, Doctor Eisenmenger, and I resent your implication otherwise. Just because I think that Doctor Woodforde was wrong doesn't mean that I am not trying to discover why this trust has an apparent excess of deaths."

"It's more than an 'apparent' excess." In truth, Eisenmenger was taken by surprise by the chief executive's reaction. He added defiantly, "I think that she was right."

"Prove it," Greeley challenged.

"I'm not sure I can."

"Well, then, I suggest you shut up about it. If you try to make this public, we may have to consider referring you to the General Medical Council."

Chapter Fifty-Seven

"Can I have a word, Peter?"

Sulston looked angry, and no less so when he saw who was hailing him. He stopped, though. The wind in the car park whipped at his jacket as he waited for Eisenmenger to approach him. "What is it?"

"I was wondering about your relationship with Paul Dunant."

"What the fuck is that to do with you?"

"Can we speak about it?"

"Look, Eisenmenger, do you know what I'm going through at the moment?"

"No . . ."

"Let me tell you, then. Since Paul was charged, I've had to move house, I've had to ditch my mobile phone and get a temporary pay-monthly, and I can't do my job properly because the patients won't leave it alone."

"And you're an innocent in all this?"

Sulston reacted as if Eisenmenger had hit him. "Of course, I bloody am!"

Eisenmenger shook his head. "You knew, Sulston. You knew. You had to."

"What the fuck are you talking about?"

"You'd known him a long, long time."

"People can surprise you, even after years."

"Shall I tell you what I think was going on?"

Sulston stared at him as they faced each other down in the car park. He replied slowly, "I imagine you'll tell me whether I want to hear it or not . . ."

"I think that you killed people because you knew – or perhaps you just suspected – that they would fall into the hands of Frank via Paul. Of course, you couldn't tell Paul . . ."

"That would be laughable if it weren't so offensive and slanderous."

"Except that there's nobody but you and I here, so we can forget the 'slanderous'."

Sulston advanced on him. He was a little bit taller than Eisenmenger, and Eisenmenger had to tell himself that this confrontation was necessary – to himself, if not to anyone or anything else – so that he didn't back down. Sulston's finger jabbed out at the pathologist. "And you'd better not repeat the allegation in front of anyone else, Eisenmenger. If you do, I'll come down on you like a ton of bricks."

He stalked away and Eisenmenger didn't follow him.

*

Beverley was no nurse but he didn't mind. Nor was she a psychotherapist, but he talked to her anyway. She listened well, and he didn't mind the advice that she gave him.

"Give it up, John."

"But there must be a way of proving it."

"How? Most of the dead were cremated."

"Not all of them."

"You want to exhume them?"

"If we have to."

"Do you know how difficult it is to get an exhumation order, John?"

"No, but you're going to tell me, I guess."

"Fucking impossible. Especially without a lot of evidence."

"But we can't get the evidence without an exhumation . . ."

They were sitting at the kitchen table, coffee in hand, facing one another. She said, "Life's a bitch, John. Give it up."

"And let Sulston get away with it?"

She leaned back. "Why not? If what you say is true, he saved them from a far more horrible fate. One you endured yourself. One that nearly killed you."

"He killed them, Beverley. It was murder."

"Without proof, that's a meaningless statement."

"But you're a police officer."

She laughed, but it wasn't full of warmth. Draining her

coffee, she said, "That's exactly right, John. I'm a police officer." She stood, as if to leave the room, but then stopped and looked at him. "There's always Edward Marsham's body. I've made sure that it wasn't interred. Perhaps we can get something on Sulston from that."

"Ah . . ."

She looked at him fearfully. "Sulston killed Marsham, right?"

He said after thinking about this, "I'm not so sure."

"You're not?" She was surprised by his answer.

He shook his head. "I can't think of a reason why he should have done. Can you?"

"But, surely . . . You said about the venflons . . . You raised the possibility that he was murdered . . ."

"That's all it ever was – a possibility."

She sat again, shaking her head. "He died naturally?"

"Most probably."

"Jesus . . ." she breathed.

He shrugged. "A man can change his mind, can't he?"

*

Bayes sighed. He held Adrian in his arms and listened to the wind blowing outside the bedroom window. The quandary about his future played heavily so that he couldn't sleep. The Independent Police Complaints Commission had already interviewed him twice and it hadn't gone well in either encounter. It all struck him as flagrantly unfair; in deploying the Taser, he had saved John Eisenmenger from being horribly burned by the acid that Frank Aston was about to pour over him. He hadn't meant that his action should have such terrible consequences. He hadn't meant that Aston should be blinded. He didn't think that his action had been disproportionate, which is what the IPCC had banged on about.

Lambert hadn't been particularly supportive. He seemed to think that Bayes, a mere detective sergeant, was expendable; if he was found to be culpable and was charged with grievous bodily harm, and thereby his career was ended, then so be it. There were plenty of detective sergeants to replace him, apparently. Beverley had been more supportive, which had surprised and delighted him. She had been a witness, of course; she said that she had told the investigators that what he had done had been entirely reasonable, and he believed her. His opinion of her had rotated through one hundred and eighty degrees during the course of the case.

But too many of the others – the uniforms, the other plain clothes officers – now looked at him differently, and not nicely either. The atmosphere had changed, and not for the better. He had been aware that his personal circumstances marked him in their eyes, even in the enlightened third millennium but, now . . .

Now he was marked in an entirely different, entirely worse way.

And he wasn't sure he could cope.

Beside him, Adrian stirred and murmured something

unintelligible. It had been Adrian's view that he should quit the police and he had to admit that this seemed very attractive to him. It was, though, the nuclear option; the one from which there was no going back. He didn't quite feel ready for that.

Ironically, it was Beverley Wharton's name that he kept thinking of. He had established a professional rapport with her that he had so recently thought might prove impossible. Beverley Wharton might save him as a policeman. His arm under Adrian was aching but he didn't mind. Whatever he did, he would always have his partner. He felt that perhaps he had a partner at work. It was a novel feeling.

ENDEAVOUR INK

Endeavour Ink is an imprint of Endeavour Press.

If you enjoyed *A Kiss Before Killing* check out
Endeavour Press's eBooks here:
www.endeavourpress.com

For weekly updates on our free and discounted eBooks sign up
to our newsletter:
www.endeavourpress.com

Follow us on Twitter:
@EndeavourPress

ENDEAVOUR PRESS